I0672311

The Real Thing

and Other Stories

The Real Thing

and Other Stories

HENRY JAMES

ÆGYPAN PRESS

Texts of the 1893 London edition.

The Real Thing
A publication of
ÆGYPAN PRESS

www.aegypan.com

Table of Contents

The Real Thing 7
Sir Dominick Ferrand 31
Nona Vincent 79
The Chaperon 105
Greville Fane 141

The Real Thing

Chapter I

When the porter's wife (she used to answer the house-bell), announced "A gentleman – with a lady, sir," I had, as I often had in those days, for the wish was father to the thought, an immediate vision of sitters. Sitters my visitors in this case proved to be; but not in the sense I should have preferred. However, there was nothing at first to indicate that they might not have come for a portrait. The gentleman, a man of fifty, very high and very straight, with a moustache slightly grizzled and a dark grey walking-coat admirably fitted, both of which I noted professionally – I don't mean as a barber or yet as a tailor – would have struck me as a celebrity if celebrities often were striking. It was a truth of which I had for some time been conscious that a figure with a good deal of frontage was, as one might say, almost never a public institution. A glance at the lady helped to remind me of this paradoxical law: she also looked too distinguished to be a "personality." Moreover one would scarcely come across two variations together.

Neither of the pair spoke immediately – they only prolonged the preliminary gaze which suggested that each wished to give the other a chance. They were visibly shy; they stood there letting me take them in – which, as I afterwards perceived, was the most practical thing they could have done. In this way their embarrassment served their cause. I had seen people painfully reluctant to mention that they desired anything so gross as to be represented on canvas; but the scruples of my new friends appeared almost insurmountable. Yet the gentleman might have said "I should like a portrait of my wife," and the lady might have said "I should like a portrait of my husband." Perhaps they were not husband and wife – this naturally would make the matter more delicate. Perhaps they wished to be done together – in which case they ought to have brought a third person to break the news.

"We come from Mr. Rivet," the lady said at last, with a dim smile which had the effect of a moist sponge passed over a "sunk" piece of painting, as well as of a vague allusion to vanished beauty. She was as tall and straight, in her degree, as her companion, and with ten years less to carry. She looked as sad as a woman could look whose face was not charged with expression; that is her tinted oval mask showed friction as an exposed surface shows it. The hand of time had played over her freely, but only to simplify. She was slim and stiff, and so well-dressed, in dark blue cloth, with lappets and pockets and buttons, that it was clear she employed the same tailor as her husband. The couple had an indefinable air of prosperous thrift – they evidently got a good deal of luxury for their money. If I was to be one of their luxuries it would behoove me to consider my terms.

"Ah, Claude Rivet recommended me?" I inquired; and I added that it was very kind of him, though I could reflect that, as he only painted landscape, this was not a sacrifice.

The lady looked very hard at the gentleman, and the gentleman looked round the room. Then staring at the floor a moment and stroking his moustache, he rested his pleasant eyes on me with the remark:

"He said you were the right one."

"I try to be, when people want to sit."

"Yes, we should like to," said the lady anxiously.

"Do you mean together?"

My visitors exchanged a glance. "If you could do anything with *me*, I suppose it would be double," the gentleman stammered.

"Oh yes, there's naturally a higher charge for two figures than for one."

"We should like to make it pay," the husband confessed.

"That's very good of you," I returned, appreciating so unwonted a sympathy – for I supposed he meant pay the artist.

A sense of strangeness seemed to dawn on the lady. "We mean for the illustrations – Mr. Rivet said you might put one in."

"Put one in – an illustration?" I was equally confused.

"Sketch her off, you know," said the gentleman, coloring.

It was only then that I understood the service Claude Rivet had rendered me; he had told them that I worked in black and white, for magazines, for story-books, for sketches of contemporary life, and consequently had frequent employment for models. These things were true, but it was not less true (I may confess it now – whether because the aspiration was to lead to everything or to nothing I leave the reader to guess), that I couldn't get the honors, to say nothing of the emoluments, of a great painter of portraits out of my head. My "illustrations" were my pot-boilers; I looked to a different branch of art (far and away the most interesting it had always seemed to me), to perpetuate my fame. There was no shame in looking to it also to make my fortune; but that fortune was by so much further from being made from the moment my visitors wished to be "done" for nothing. I was disappointed; for in the pictorial sense I had immediately *seen* them. I had seized their type – I had already settled what I would do with it. Something that wouldn't absolutely have pleased them, I afterwards reflected.

"Ah, you're – you're – a – ?" I began, as soon as I had mastered my surprise. I couldn't bring out the dingy word "models"; it seemed to fit the case so little.

"We haven't had much practice," said the lady.

"We've got to *do* something, and we've thought that an artist in your line might perhaps make something of us," her husband threw off. He further mentioned that they didn't know many artists and that they had gone first, on the off-chance (he painted views of course, but sometimes put in figures – perhaps I remembered), to Mr. Rivet, whom they had met a few years before at a place in Norfolk where he was sketching.

"We used to sketch a little ourselves," the lady hinted.

"It's very awkward, but we absolutely *must* do something," her husband went on.

"Of course, we're not so *very* young," she admitted, with a wan smile.

With the remark that I might as well know something more about them, the husband had handed me a card extracted from a neat new pocketbook (their appurtenances were all of the freshest) and inscribed with the words "Major Monarch." Impressive as these words were they didn't carry my knowledge much further; but my visitor presently added: "I've left the army, and we've had the misfortune to lose our money. In fact our means are dreadfully small."

"It's an awful bore," said Mrs. Monarch.

They evidently wished to be discreet – to take care not to swagger because they were gentlefolks. I perceived they would have been willing to recognize this as something of a drawback, at the same time that I guessed at an underlying sense – their consolation in adversity – that they *had* their points. They certainly had; but these advantages struck me as preponderantly social; such for instance as would help to make a drawing room look well. However, a drawing room was always, or ought to be, a picture.

In consequence of his wife's allusion to their age Major Monarch observed: "Naturally, it's more for the figure that we thought of going in. We can still hold ourselves up." On the instant I saw that the figure was indeed their strong point. His "naturally" didn't sound vain, but it lighted up the question. "*She* has got the best," he continued, nodding at his wife, with a pleasant after-dinner absence of circumlocution. I could only reply, as if we were in fact sitting over our wine, that this didn't prevent his own from being very good; which led him in turn to rejoin: "We thought that if you ever have to do people like us, we might be something like it. *She*, particularly – for a lady in a book, you know."

I was so amused by them that, to get more of it, I did my best to take their point of view; and though it was an embarrassment to find myself appraising physically, as if they were animals on hire or useful blacks, a pair whom I should have expected to meet only in one of the relations in which criticism is tacit, I looked at Mrs. Monarch judicially enough to be able to exclaim, after a moment, with conviction: "Oh yes, a lady in a book!" She was singularly like a bad illustration.

"We'll stand up, if you like," said the Major; and he raised himself before me with a really grand air.

I could take his measure at a glance – he was six feet two and a perfect gentleman. It would have paid any club in process of formation and in want of a stamp to engage him at a salary to stand in the principal window. What struck me immediately was that in coming to me they had rather missed their vocation; they could surely have been turned to better account for advertising purposes. I couldn't of course see the thing in detail, but I could see them make someone's fortune – I don't mean their own. There was something in them for a waistcoat-maker, an hotel-keeper or a soap-vendor. I could imagine "We always use it" pinned on their bosoms with the greatest effect; I had a vision of the promptitude with which they would launch a table d'hôte.

Mrs. Monarch sat still, not from pride but from shyness, and presently her husband said to her: "Get up my dear and show how smart you are." She obeyed, but she had no need to get up to show it. She walked to the end of the studio, and then she came back blushing, with her fluttered eyes on her husband. I was reminded of an incident I had accidentally had a glimpse of in Paris – being with a friend there, a dramatist about to produce a play – when an actress came to him to ask to be entrusted with a part. She went through her paces before him, walked up and down as Mrs. Monarch was doing. Mrs. Monarch did it quite as well, but I abstained from applauding. It was very odd to see such people apply for such poor pay. She looked as if she had ten thousand a year. Her husband had used the word that described her: she was, in the London current jargon, essentially and typically "smart." Her figure was, in the same order of ideas, conspicuously and irreproachably "good." For a woman of her age her waist was surprisingly small;

her elbow moreover had the orthodox crook. She held her head at the conventional angle; but why did she come to *me?* She ought to have tried on jackets at a big shop. I feared my visitors were not only destitute, but "artistic" – which would be a great complication. When she sat down again I thanked her, observing that what a draughtsman most valued in his model was the faculty of keeping quiet.

"Oh, *she* can keep quiet," said Major Monarch. Then he added, jocosely: "I've always kept her quiet."

"I'm not a nasty fidget, am I?" Mrs. Monarch appealed to her husband.

He addressed his answer to me. "Perhaps it isn't out of place to mention – because we ought to be quite businesslike, oughtn't we? – that when I married her she was known as the Beautiful Statue."

"Oh dear!" said Mrs. Monarch, ruefully.

"Of course I should want a certain amount of expression," I rejoined.

"Of *course!*" they both exclaimed.

"And then I suppose you know that you'll get awfully tired."

"Oh, we *never* get tired!" they eagerly cried.

"Have you had any kind of practice?"

They hesitated – they looked at each other. "We've been photographed, *immensely,*" said Mrs. Monarch.

"She means the fellows have asked us," added the Major.

"I see – because you're so good-looking."

"I don't know what they thought, but they were always after us."

"We always got our photographs for nothing," smiled Mrs. Monarch.

"We might have brought some, my dear," her husband remarked.

"I'm not sure we have any left. We've given quantities away," she explained to me.

"With our autographs and that sort of thing," said the Major.

"Are they to be got in the shops?" I inquired, as a harmless pleasantry.

"Oh, yes; hers – they used to be."

"Not now," said Mrs. Monarch, with her eyes on the floor.

Chapter II

I could fancy the "sort of thing" they put on the presentation-copies of their photographs, and I was sure they wrote a beautiful hand. It was odd how quickly I was sure of everything that concerned them. If they were now so poor as to have to earn shillings and pence, they never had had much of a margin. Their good looks had been their capital, and they had good-humoredly made the most of the career that this resource marked out for them. It was in their faces, the blankness, the deep intellectual repose of the twenty years of country-house visiting which had given them pleasant intonations. I could see the sunny drawing rooms, sprinkled with periodicals she didn't read, in which Mrs. Monarch had continuously sat; I could see the wet shrubberies in which she had walked, equipped to admiration for either exercise. I could see the rich covers the Major had helped to shoot and the wonderful garments in which, late at night, he repaired to the smoking-room to talk about them. I could imagine their leggings and waterproofs, their knowing tweeds and rugs, their rolls of sticks and cases of tackle and neat umbrellas; and I could evoke the exact appearance of their servants and the compact variety of their luggage on the platforms of country stations.

They gave small tips, but they were liked; they didn't do anything themselves, but they were welcome. They looked so well everywhere; they gratified the general relish for stature, complexion and "form." They knew it without fatuity or vulgarity, and they respected themselves in consequence. They were not superficial; they were thorough and kept themselves up – it had been their line. People with such a taste for activity had to have some line. I could feel how, even in a dull house, they could have been counted upon for cheerfulness. At present something had happened – it didn't matter what, their little income had grown less, it had grown least – and they had to do something for pocket-money. Their friends liked them, but didn't like to support them. There was something about them that represented credit – their clothes, their manners, their type; but if credit is a large empty pocket in which an occasional chink reverberates, the chink at least must be audible. What they wanted of me was to help to make it so. Fortunately they had no children – I soon divined that. They would also perhaps wish our relations to be kept secret: this was why it was "for the figure" – the reproduction of the face would betray them.

I liked them – they were so simple; and I had no objection to them if they would suit. But, somehow, with all their perfections I didn't easily believe in them. After all they were amateurs, and the ruling passion of my life was the detestation of the amateur. Combined with this was another perversity – an innate preference for the represented subject over the real one: the defect of the real one was so apt to be a lack of representation. I liked things that appeared; then one was sure. Whether they *were* or not was a subordinate and almost always a profitless question. There were other considerations, the first of which was that I already had two or three people in use, notably a young person with big feet, in alpaca, from Kilburn, who for a couple of years had come to me regularly for my illustrations and with whom I was still – perhaps ignobly – satisfied. I frankly explained to my visitors how the case stood; but they had taken more precautions than I supposed. They had reasoned out their opportunity, for Claude Rivet had told them of the projected edition deluxe of one of the writers of our day – the rarest of the novelists – who, long neglected by the multitudinous vulgar and dearly prized by the attentive (need I mention Philip Vincent?) had had the happy fortune of seeing, late in life, the dawn and then the full light of a higher criticism – an estimate in which, on the part of the public, there was something really of expiation. The edition in question, planned by a publisher of taste, was practically an act of high reparation; the wood-cuts with which it was to be enriched were the homage of English art to one of the most independent representatives of English letters. Major and Mrs. Monarch confessed to me that they had hoped I might be able to work *them* into my share of the enterprise. They knew I was to do the first of the books, "Rutland Ramsay," but I had to make clear to them that my participation in the rest of the affair – this first book was to be a test – was to depend on the satisfaction I should give. If this should be limited my employers would drop me without a scruple. It was therefore a crisis for me, and naturally I was making special preparations, looking about for new people, if they should be necessary, and securing the best types. I admitted however that I should like to settle down to two or three good models who would do for everything.

"Should we have often to – a – put on special clothes?" Mrs. Monarch timidly demanded.

"Dear, yes – that's half the business."

"And should we be expected to supply our own costumes?"

"Oh, no; I've got a lot of things. A painter's models put on – or put off – anything he likes."

"And do you mean – a – the same?"

"The same?"

Mrs. Monarch looked at her husband again.

"Oh, she was just wondering," he explained, "if the costumes are in *general* use." I had to confess that they were, and I mentioned further that some of them (I had a lot of genuine, greasy last-century things), had served their time, a hundred years ago, on living, world-stained men and women. "We'll put on anything that fits," said the Major.

"Oh, I arrange that – they fit in the pictures."

"I'm afraid I should do better for the modern books. I would come as you like," said Mrs. Monarch.

"She has got a lot of clothes at home: they might do for contemporary life," her husband continued.

"Oh, I can fancy scenes in which you'd be quite natural." And indeed I could see the slipshod rearrangements of stale properties – the stories I tried to produce pictures for without the exasperation of reading them – whose sandy tracts the good lady might help to people. But I had to return to the fact that for this sort of work – the daily mechanical grind – I was already equipped; the people I was working with were fully adequate.

"We only thought we might be more like *some* characters," said Mrs. Monarch mildly, getting up.

Her husband also rose; he stood looking at me with a dim wistfulness that was touching in so fine a man. "Wouldn't it be rather a pull sometimes to have – a – to have – ?" He hung fire; he wanted me to help him by phrasing what he meant. But I couldn't – I didn't know. So he brought it out, awkwardly: "The *real* thing; a gentleman, you know, or a lady." I was quite ready to give a general assent – I admitted that there was a great deal in that. This encouraged Major Monarch to say, following up his appeal with an unacted gulp: "It's awfully hard – we've tried everything." The gulp was communicative; it proved too much for his wife. Before I knew it Mrs. Monarch had dropped again upon a divan and burst into tears. Her husband sat down beside her, holding one of her hands; whereupon she quickly dried her eyes with the other, while I felt embarrassed as she looked up at me. "There isn't a confounded job I haven't applied for – waited for – prayed for. You can fancy we'd be pretty bad first. Secretaryships and that sort of thing? You might as well ask for a peerage. I'd be *anything* – I'm strong; a messenger or a coalheaver. I'd put on a gold-laced cap and open carriage-doors in front of the haberdasher's; I'd hang about a station, to carry portmanteaus; I'd be a postman. But they won't *look* at you; there are thousands, as good as yourself, already on the ground. *Gentlemen,* poor beggars, who have drunk their wine, who have kept their hunters!"

I was as reassuring as I knew how to be, and my visitors were presently on their feet again while, for the experiment, we agreed on an hour. We were discussing it when the door opened and Miss Churm came in with a wet umbrella. Miss Churm had to take the omnibus to Maida Vale and then walk half-a-mile. She looked a trifle blowsy and slightly splashed. I scarcely ever saw her come in without thinking afresh how odd it was that, being so little in herself, she should yet be so much in others. She was a meager little Miss Churm, but she was an ample heroine of romance. She was only a freckled cockney, but she could represent everything, from a fine lady to a shepherdess; she had the faculty, as she might have had a fine voice or long hair.

She couldn't spell, and she loved beer, but she had two or three "points," and practice, and a knack, and mother-wit, and a kind of whimsical sensibility, and a love of the theater, and seven sisters, and not an ounce of respect, especially for the H. The first thing my visitors saw was that her umbrella was wet, and in their spotless perfection they visibly winced at it. The rain had come on since their arrival.

"I'm all in a soak; there *was* a mess of people in the 'bus. I wish you lived near a stytion," said Miss Churm. I requested her to get ready as quickly as possible, and she passed into the room in which she always changed her dress. But before going out she asked me what she was to get into this time.

"It's the Russian princess, don't you know?" I answered; "the one with the 'golden eyes,' in black velvet, for the long thing in the Cheapside."

"Golden eyes? I *say!*" cried Miss Churm, while my companions watched her with intensity as she withdrew. She always arranged herself, when she was late, before I could turn round; and I kept my visitors a little, on purpose, so that they might get an idea, from seeing her, what would be expected of themselves. I mentioned that she was quite my notion of an excellent model – she was really very clever.

"Do you think she looks like a Russian princess?" Major Monarch asked, with lurking alarm.

"When I make her, yes."

"Oh, if you have to *make* her – !" he reasoned, acutely.

"That's the most you can ask. There are so many that are not makeable."

"Well now, *here's* a lady" – and with a persuasive smile he passed his arm into his wife's – "who's already made!"

"Oh, I'm not a Russian princess," Mrs. Monarch protested, a little coldly. I could see that she had known some and didn't like them. There, immediately, was a complication of a kind that I never had to fear with Miss Churm.

This young lady came back in black velvet – the gown was rather rusty and very low on her lean shoulders – and with a Japanese fan in her red hands. I reminded her that in the scene I was doing she had to look over someone's head. "I forget whose it is; but it doesn't matter. Just look over a head."

"I'd rather look over a stove," said Miss Churm; and she took her station near the fire. She fell into position, settled herself into a tall attitude, gave a certain backward inclination to her head and a certain forward droop to her fan, and looked, at least to my prejudiced sense, distinguished and charming, foreign and dangerous. We left her looking so, while I went downstairs with Major and Mrs. Monarch.

"I think I could come about as near it as that," said Mrs. Monarch.

"Oh, you think she's shabby, but you must allow for the alchemy of art."

However, they went off with an evident increase of comfort, founded on their demonstrable advantage in being the real thing. I could fancy them shuddering over Miss Churm. She was very droll about them when I went back, for I told her what they wanted.

"Well, if *she* can sit I'll tyke to bookkeeping," said my model.

"She's very ladylike," I replied, as an innocent form of aggravation.

"So much the worse for *you.* That means she can't turn round."

"She'll do for the fashionable novels."

"Oh yes, she'll *do* for them!" my model humorously declared. "Ain't they had enough without her?" I had often sociably denounced them to Miss Churm.

Chapter III

It was for the elucidation of a mystery in one of these works that I first tried Mrs. Monarch. Her husband came with her, to be useful if necessary – it was sufficiently clear that as a general thing he would prefer to come with her. At first I wondered if this were for "propriety's" sake – if he were going to be jealous and meddling. The idea was too tiresome, and if it had been confirmed it would speedily have brought our acquaintance to a close. But I soon saw there was nothing in it and that if he accompanied Mrs. Monarch it was (in addition to the chance of being wanted), simply because he had nothing else to do. When she was away from him his occupation was gone – she never *had* been away from him. I judged, rightly, that in their awkward situation their close union was their main comfort and that this union had no weak spot. It was a real marriage, an encouragement to the hesitating, a nut for pessimists to crack. Their address was humble (I remember afterwards thinking it had been the only thing about them that was really professional), and I could fancy the lamentable lodgings in which the Major would have been left alone. He could bear them with his wife – he couldn't bear them without her.

He had too much tact to try and make himself agreeable when he couldn't be useful; so he simply sat and waited, when I was too absorbed in my work to talk. But I liked to make him talk – it made my work, when it didn't interrupt it, less sordid, less special. To listen to him was to combine the excitement of going out with the economy of staying at home. There was only one hindrance: that I seemed not to know any of the people he and his wife had known. I think he wondered extremely, during the term of our intercourse, whom the deuce I *did* know. He hadn't a stray sixpence of an idea to fumble for; so we didn't spin it very fine – we confined ourselves to questions of leather and even of liquor (saddlers and breeches-makers and how to get good claret cheap), and matters like "good trains" and the habits of small game. His lore on these last subjects was astonishing, he managed to interweave the station-master with the ornithologist. When he couldn't talk about greater things he could talk cheerfully about smaller, and since I couldn't accompany him into reminiscences of the fashionable world he could lower the conversation without a visible effort to my level.

So earnest a desire to please was touching in a man who could so easily have knocked one down. He looked after the fire and had an opinion on the draught of the stove, without my asking him, and I could see that he thought many of my arrangements not half clever enough. I remember telling him that if I were only rich I would offer him a salary to come and teach me how to live. Sometimes he gave a random sigh, of which the essence was: "Give me even such a bare old barrack as *this*, and I'd do something with it!" When I wanted to use him he came alone; which was an illustration of the superior courage of women. His wife could bear her solitary second floor, and she was in general more discreet; showing by various small reserves that she was alive to the propriety of keeping our relations markedly professional – not letting them slide into sociability. She wished it to remain clear that she and the Major were employed, not cultivated, and if she approved of me as a superior, who could be kept in his place, she never thought me quite good enough for an equal.

She sat with great intensity, giving the whole of her mind to it, and was capable of remaining for an hour almost as motionless as if she were before a photographer's lens. I could see she had been photographed often, but somehow the very habit that made her good for that purpose unfitted her for mine. At first I was extremely pleased with her ladylike air, and it was a satisfaction, on coming to follow her lines, to see how good they were and how far they could lead the pencil. But after a few times I began to find her too insurmountably stiff; do what I would with it my drawing looked like a photograph or a copy of a photograph. Her figure had no variety of expression – she herself had no sense of variety. You may say that this was my business, was only a question of placing her. I placed her in every conceivable position, but she managed to obliterate their differences. She was always a lady certainly, and into the bargain was always the same lady. She was the real thing, but always the same thing. There were moments when I was oppressed by the serenity of her confidence that she *was* the real thing. All her dealings with me and all her husband's were an implication that this was lucky for *me*. Meanwhile I found myself trying to invent types that approached her own, instead of making her own transform itself – in the clever way that was not impossible, for instance, to poor Miss Churm. Arrange as I would and take the precautions I would, she always, in my pictures, came out too tall – landing me in the dilemma of having represented a fascinating woman as seven feet high, which, out of respect perhaps to my own very much scantier inches, was far from my idea of such a personage.

The case was worse with the Major – nothing I could do would keep *him* down, so that he became useful only for the representation of brawny giants. I adored variety and range, I cherished human accidents, the illustrative note; I wanted to characterize closely, and the thing in the world I most hated was the danger of being ridden by a type. I had quarreled with some of my friends about it – I had parted company with them for maintaining that one *had* to be, and that if the type was beautiful (witness Raphael and Leonardo), the servitude was only a gain. I was neither Leonardo nor Raphael; I might only be a presumptuous young modern searcher, but I held that everything was to be sacrificed sooner than character. When they averred that the haunting type in question could easily *be* character, I retorted, perhaps superficially: "Whose?" It couldn't be everybody's – it might end in being nobody's.

After I had drawn Mrs. Monarch a dozen times I perceived more clearly than before that the value of such a model as Miss Churm resided precisely in the fact that she had no positive stamp, combined of course with the other fact that what she did have was a curious and inexplicable talent for imitation. Her usual appearance was like a curtain which she could draw up at request for a capital performance. This performance was simply suggestive; but it was a word to the wise – it was vivid and pretty. Sometimes, even, I thought it, though she was plain herself, too insipidly pretty; I made it a reproach to her that the figures drawn from her were monotonously (betement, as we used to say) graceful. Nothing made her more angry: it was so much her pride to feel that she could sit for characters that had nothing in common with each other. She would accuse me at such moments of taking away her "reputytion."

It suffered a certain shrinkage, this queer quantity, from the repeated visits of my new friends. Miss Churm was greatly in demand, never in want of employment, so I had no scruple in putting her off occasionally, to try them more at my ease. It was certainly amusing at first to do the real thing – it was amusing to do Major Monarch's trousers. They *were* the real thing, even if he did come out colossal. It was amusing to do his wife's back hair (it was so mathematically neat,) and the particular "smart" tension of her tight stays. She lent herself especially to positions in which the face was somewhat averted or blurred; she abounded in ladylike back views and *profils perdus.* When she stood erect she took naturally one of the attitudes in which court-painters represent queens and princesses; so that I found myself wondering whether, to draw out this accomplishment, I couldn't get the editor of the Cheapside to publish a really royal romance, "A Tale of Buckingham Palace." Sometimes, however, the real thing and the make-believe came into contact; by which I mean that Miss Churm, keeping an appointment or coming to make one on days when I had much work in hand, encountered her invidious rivals. The encounter was not on their part, for they noticed her no more than if she had been the housemaid; not from intentional loftiness, but simply because, as yet, professionally, they didn't know how to fraternize, as I could guess that they would have liked – or at least that the Major would. They couldn't talk about the omnibus – they always walked; and they didn't know what else to try – she wasn't interested in good trains or cheap claret. Besides, they must have felt – in the air – that she was amused at them, secretly derisive of their ever knowing how. She was not a person to conceal her skepticism if she had had a chance to show it. On the other hand Mrs. Monarch didn't think her tidy; for why else did she take pains to say to me (it was going out of the way, for Mrs. Monarch), that she didn't like dirty women?

One day when my young lady happened to be present with my other sitters (she even dropped in, when it was convenient, for a chat), I asked her to be so good as to lend a hand in getting tea – a service with which she was familiar and which was one of a class that, living as I did in a small way, with slender domestic resources, I often appealed to my models to render. They liked to lay hands on my property, to break the sitting, and sometimes the china – I made them feel Bohemian. The next time I saw Miss Churm after this incident she surprised me greatly by making a scene about it – she accused me of having wished to humiliate her. She had not resented the outrage at the time, but had seemed obliging and amused, enjoying the comedy of asking Mrs. Monarch, who sat vague and silent, whether she would have cream and sugar, and putting an exaggerated simper into the question. She had tried intonations – as if she too wished to pass for the real thing; till I was afraid my other visitors would take offence.

Oh, *they* were determined not to do this; and their touching patience was the measure of their great need. They would sit by the hour, uncomplaining, till I was ready to use them; they would come back on the chance of being wanted and would walk away cheerfully if they were not. I used to go to the door with them to see in what magnificent order they retreated. I tried to find other employment for them – I introduced them to several artists. But they didn't "take," for reasons I could appreciate, and I became conscious, rather anxiously, that after such disappointments they fell back upon me with a heavier weight. They did me the honor to think that it was I who was most *their* form. They were not picturesque enough for the painters, and in those days there were not so many serious workers in black and white. Besides, they had an eye to the great job I had mentioned to them – they had secretly set their hearts on supplying the right essence for my pictorial vindication of our fine novelist. They knew that for this undertaking I should want no costume-effects, none of the frippery of past ages – that it was a case in which everything would be contemporary and satirical and, presumably, genteel. If I could work them into it their future would be assured, for the labor would of course be long and the occupation steady.

One day Mrs. Monarch came without her husband – she explained his absence by his having had to go to the City. While she sat there in her usual anxious stiffness there came, at the door, a knock which I immediately recognized as the subdued appeal of a model out of work. It was followed by the entrance of a young man whom I easily perceived to be a foreigner and who proved in fact an Italian acquainted with no English word but my name, which he uttered in a way that made it seem to include all others. I had not then visited his country, nor was I proficient in his tongue; but as he was not so meanly constituted – what Italian is? – as to depend only on that member for expression he conveyed to me, in familiar but graceful mimicry, that he was in search of exactly the employment in which the lady before me was engaged. I was not struck with him at first, and while I continued to draw I emitted rough sounds of discouragement and dismissal. He stood his ground, however, not importunately, but with a dumb, doglike fidelity in his eyes which amounted to innocent impudence – the manner of a devoted servant (he might have been in the house for years), unjustly suspected. Suddenly I saw that this very attitude and expression made a picture, whereupon I told him to sit down and wait till I should be free. There was another picture in the way he obeyed me, and I observed as I worked that there were others still in the way he looked wonderingly, with his head thrown back, about the high studio. He might have been crossing himself in St. Peter's. Before I finished I said to myself: "The fellow's a bankrupt orange-monger, but he's a treasure."

When Mrs. Monarch withdrew he passed across the room like a flash to open the door for her, standing there with the rapt, pure gaze of the young Dante spellbound by the young Beatrice. As I never insisted, in such situations, on the blankness of the British domestic, I reflected that he had the making of a servant (and I needed one, but couldn't pay him to be only that), as well as of a model; in short I made up my mind to adopt my bright adventurer if he would agree to officiate in the double capacity. He jumped at my offer, and in the event my rashness (for I had known nothing about him), was not brought home to me. He proved a sympathetic though a desultory ministrant, and had in a wonderful degree the sentiment de la pose. It was uncultivated, instinctive; a part of the happy instinct which had guided him to my door and helped him to spell out my name on the card nailed to it. He had had no other introduction to me than a guess, from the shape of my high north window, seen outside, that my place was a studio and that as a studio it would contain an artist. He had wandered to England in search of fortune, like other itinerants, and had embarked, with a partner and a small green handcart, on the sale of penny ices. The ices had melted away and the partner had dissolved in their train. My young man wore tight yellow trousers with reddish stripes and his name was Oronte. He was sallow but fair, and when I put him into some old clothes of my own he looked like an Englishman. He was as good as Miss Churm, who could look, when required, like an Italian.

Chapter IV

I thought Mrs. Monarch's face slightly convulsed when, on her coming back with her husband, she found Oronte installed. It was strange to have to recognize in a scrap of a *lazzarone* a competitor to her magnificent Major. It was she who scented danger first, for the Major was anecdotically unconscious. But Oronte gave us tea, with a hundred eager confusions (he had never seen such a queer process), and I think she thought better of me for having at last an "establishment." They saw a couple of drawings that I had made of the establishment, and Mrs. Monarch hinted that it never would have struck her that he had sat for them. "Now the drawings you make from *us*, they look exactly like us," she reminded me, smiling in triumph; and I recognized that this was indeed just their defect. When I drew the Monarchs I couldn't, somehow, get away from them – get into the character I wanted to represent; and I had not the least desire my model should be discoverable in my picture. Miss Churm never was, and Mrs. Monarch thought I hid her, very properly, because she was vulgar; whereas if she was lost it was only as the dead who go to heaven are lost – in the gain of an angel the more.

By this time I had got a certain start with "Rutland Ramsay," the first novel in the great projected series; that is I had produced a dozen drawings, several with the help of the Major and his wife, and I had sent them in for approval. My understanding with the publishers, as I have already hinted, had been that I was to be left to do my work, in this particular case, as I liked, with the whole book committed to me; but my connection with the rest of the series was only contingent. There were moments when, frankly, it *was* a comfort to have the real thing under one's hand; for there were characters in "Rutland Ramsay" that were very much like it. There were people presumably as straight as the Major and women of as good a fashion as Mrs. Monarch. There was a great deal of country-house life – treated, it is true, in a fine, fanciful, ironical, generalized way – and there was a considerable implication of knickerbockers and kilts. There were certain things I had to settle at the outset; such things for instance as the exact appearance of the hero, the particular bloom of the heroine. The author of course gave me a lead, but there was a margin for interpretation. I took the Monarchs into my confidence, I told them frankly what I was about, I mentioned my embarrassments and alternatives. "Oh, take *him!*" Mrs. Monarch murmured sweetly, looking at her husband; and "What could you want better than my wife?" the Major inquired, with the comfortable candor that now prevailed between us.

I was not obliged to answer these remarks – I was only obliged to place my sitters. I was not easy in mind, and I postponed, a little timidly perhaps, the solution of the question. The book was a large canvas, the other figures were numerous, and I worked off at first some of the episodes in which the hero and the heroine were not concerned. When once I had set *them* up I should have to stick to them – I couldn't make my young man seven feet high in one place and five feet nine in another. I inclined on the whole to the latter measurement, though the Major more than once reminded me that *he* looked about as young as anyone. It was indeed quite possible to arrange him, for the figure, so that it would have been difficult to detect his age. After the spontaneous Oronte had been with me a month, and after I had given him to understand several different times that his native exuberance would presently constitute an insurmountable barrier to our further intercourse, I waked to a sense of his heroic capacity. He was only five feet seven, but the remaining inches were latent. I tried him almost secretly at first, for I was really rather afraid of the judgment my other models would pass on such a choice. If they regarded Miss Churm as little better than a snare, what would they think of the representation by a person so little the real thing as an Italian street-vendor of a protagonist formed by a public school?

If I went a little in fear of them it was not because they bullied me, because they had got an oppressive foothold, but because in their really pathetic decorum and mysteriously permanent newness they counted on me so intensely. I was therefore very glad when Jack Hawley came home: he was always of such good counsel. He painted badly himself, but there was no one like him for putting his finger on the place. He had been absent from England for a year; he had been somewhere – I don't remember where – to get a fresh eye. I was in a good deal of dread of any such organ, but we were old friends; he had been away for months and a sense of emptiness was creeping into my life. I hadn't dodged a missile for a year.

He came back with a fresh eye, but with the same old black velvet blouse, and the first evening he spent in my studio we smoked cigarettes till the small hours. He had done no work himself, he had only got the eye; so the field was clear for the production of my little things. He wanted to see what I had done for the Cheapside, but he was disappointed in the exhibition. That at least seemed the meaning of two or three comprehensive groans which, as he lounged on my big divan, on a folded leg, looking at my latest drawings, issued from his lips with the smoke of the cigarette.

"What's the matter with you?" I asked.

"What's the matter with *you*?"

"Nothing save that I'm mystified."

"You are indeed. You're quite off the hinge. What's the meaning of this new fad?" And he tossed me, with visible irreverence, a drawing in which I happened to have depicted both my majestic models. I asked if he didn't think it good, and he replied that it struck him as execrable, given the sort of thing I had always represented myself to him as wishing to arrive at; but I let that pass, I was so anxious to see exactly what he meant. The two figures in the picture looked colossal, but I supposed this was *not* what he meant, inasmuch as, for aught he knew to the contrary, I might have been trying for that. I maintained that I was working exactly in the same way as when he last had done me the honor to commend me. "Well, there's a big hole somewhere," he answered; "wait a bit and I'll discover it." I depended upon him to do so: where else was the fresh eye? But he produced at last nothing more luminous than "I don't know – I don't like your types." This was lame, for a critic who had never consented to discuss with me anything but the question of execution, the direction of strokes and the mystery of values.

"In the drawings you've been looking at I think my types are very handsome."

"Oh, they won't do!"

"I've had a couple of new models."

"I see you have. *They* won't do."

"Are you very sure of that?"

"Absolutely – they're stupid."

"You mean *I* am – for I ought to get round that."

"You *can't* – with such people. Who are they?"

I told him, as far as was necessary, and he declared, heartlessly: *"Ce sont des gens qu'il faut mettre a la porte."*

"You've never seen them; they're awfully good," I compassionately objected.

"Not seen them? Why, all this recent work of yours drops to pieces with them. It's all I want to see of them."

"No one else has said anything against it – the Cheapside people are pleased."

"Everyone else is an ass, and the Cheapside people the biggest asses of all. Come, don't pretend, at this time of day, to have pretty illusions about the public, especially about publishers and editors. It's not for *such* animals you work – it's for those who know, *coloro che sanno;* so keep straight for *me* if you can't keep straight for yourself. There's a certain sort of thing you tried for from the first – and a very good thing it is. But this twaddle isn't *in* it." When I talked with Hawley later about "Rutland Ramsay" and its possible successors he declared that I must get back into my boat again or I would go to the bottom. His voice in short was the voice of warning.

I noted the warning, but I didn't turn my friends out of doors. They bored me a good deal; but the very fact that they bored me admonished me not to sacrifice them – if there was anything to be done with them – simply to irritation. As I look back at this phase they seem to me to have pervaded my life not a little. I have a vision of them as most of the time in my studio, seated, against the wall, on an old velvet bench to be out of the way, and looking like a pair of patient courtiers in a royal antechamber. I am convinced that during the coldest weeks of the winter they held their ground because it saved them fire. Their newness was losing its gloss, and it was impossible not to feel that they were objects of charity. Whenever Miss Churm arrived they went away, and after I was fairly launched in "Rutland Ramsay" Miss Churm arrived pretty often. They managed to express to me tacitly that they supposed I wanted her for the low life of the book, and I let them suppose it, since they had attempted to study the work – it was lying about the studio – without discovering that it dealt only with the highest circles. They had dipped into the most brilliant of our novelists without deciphering many passages. I still took an hour from them, now and again, in spite of Jack Hawley's warning: it would be time enough to dismiss them, if dismissal should be necessary, when the rigor of the season was over. Hawley had made their acquaintance – he had met them at my fireside – and thought them a ridiculous pair. Learning that he was a painter they tried to approach him, to show him too that they were the real thing; but he looked at them, across the big room, as if they were miles away: they were a compendium of everything that he most objected to in the social system of his country. Such people as that, all convention and patent-leather, with ejaculations that stopped conversation, had no business in a studio. A studio was a place to learn to see, and how could you see through a pair of feather beds?

The main inconvenience I suffered at their hands was that, at first, I was shy of letting them discover how my artful little servant had begun to sit to me for "Rutland Ramsay." They knew that I had been odd enough (they were prepared by this time to allow oddity to artists,) to pick a foreign vagabond out of the streets, when I might have had a person with whiskers and credentials; but it was some time before they learned how high I rated his accomplishments. They found him in an attitude more than once, but they never doubted I was doing him as an organ-grinder. There were several things they never guessed, and one of them was that for a striking scene in the novel, in which a footman briefly figured, it occurred to me to make use of Major Monarch as the menial. I kept putting this off, I didn't like to ask him to don the livery – besides the difficulty of finding a livery to fit him. At last, one day late in the winter, when I was at work on the despised Oronte (he caught one's idea in an instant), and was in the glow of feeling that I was going very straight, they came in, the Major and his wife, with their society laugh about nothing (there was less and less to laugh at), like country-callers – they always reminded me of that – who have walked across the park after church and are presently persuaded to stay to luncheon. Luncheon was over, but they could stay to tea – I knew they wanted it. The fit was on me, however, and I couldn't let my ardor cool and my work wait, with the fading daylight, while my model prepared it. So I asked Mrs. Monarch if she would mind laying it out – a request which, for an instant, brought all the blood to her face. Her eyes were on her husband's for a second, and some mute telegraphy passed between them. Their folly was over the next instant; his cheerful shrewdness put an end to it. So far from pitying their wounded pride, I must add, I was moved to give it as complete a lesson as I could. They bustled about together and got out the cups and saucers and made the kettle boil. I know they felt as if they were waiting on my servant, and when the tea was prepared

I said: "He'll have a cup, please – he's tired." Mrs. Monarch brought him one where he stood, and he took it from her as if he had been a gentleman at a party, squeezing a crush-hat with an elbow.

Then it came over me that she had made a great effort for me – made it with a kind of nobleness – and that I owed her a compensation. Each time I saw her after this I wondered what the compensation could be. I couldn't go on doing the wrong thing to oblige them. Oh, it *was* the wrong thing, the stamp of the work for which they sat – Hawley was not the only person to say it now. I sent in a large number of the drawings I had made for "Rutland Ramsay," and I received a warning that was more to the point than Hawley's. The artistic adviser of the house for which I was working was of opinion that many of my illustrations were not what had been looked for. Most of these illustrations were the subjects in which the Monarchs had figured. Without going into the question of what *had* been looked for, I saw at this rate I shouldn't get the other books to do. I hurled myself in despair upon Miss Churm, I put her through all her paces. I not only adopted Oronte publicly as my hero, but one morning when the Major looked in to see if I didn't require him to finish a figure for the Cheapside, for which he had begun to sit the week before, I told him that I had changed my mind – I would do the drawing from my man. At this my visitor turned pale and stood looking at me. "Is *he* your idea of an English gentleman?" he asked.

I was disappointed, I was nervous, I wanted to get on with my work; so I replied with irritation: "Oh, my dear Major – I can't be ruined for *you!*"

He stood another moment; then, without a word, he quitted the studio. I drew a long breath when he was gone, for I said to myself that I shouldn't see him again. I had not told him definitely that I was in danger of having my work rejected, but I was vexed at his not having felt the catastrophe in the air, read with me the moral of our fruitless collaboration, the lesson that, in the deceptive atmosphere of art, even the highest respectability may fail of being plastic.

I didn't owe my friends money, but I did see them again. They re-appeared together, three days later, and under the circumstances there was something tragic in the fact. It was a proof to me that they could find nothing else in life to do. They had threshed the matter out in a dismal conference – they had digested the bad news that they were not in for the series. If they were not useful to me even for the Cheapside their function seemed difficult to determine, and I could only judge at first that they had come, forgivingly, decorously, to take a last leave. This made me rejoice in secret that I had little leisure for a scene; for I had placed both my other models in position together and I was pegging away at a drawing from which I hoped to derive glory. It had been suggested by the passage in which Rutland Ramsay, drawing up a chair to Artemisia's piano-stool, says extraordinary things to her while she ostensibly fingers out a difficult piece of music. I had done Miss Churm at the piano before – it was an attitude in which she knew how to take on an absolutely poetic grace. I wished the two figures to "compose" together, intensely, and my little Italian had entered perfectly into my conception. The pair were vividly before me, the piano had been pulled out; it was a charming picture of blended youth and murmured love, which I had only to catch and keep. My visitors stood and looked at it, and I was friendly to them over my shoulder.

They made no response, but I was used to silent company and went on with my work, only a little disconcerted (even though exhilarated by the sense that *this* was at least the ideal thing), at not having got rid of them after all. Presently I heard Mrs. Monarch's sweet voice beside, or rather above me: "I wish her hair was a little better done." I looked up and she was staring with a strange fixedness at Miss Churm, whose back was turned to her. "Do you mind my just touching it?" she went on – a question which made me spring up for an instant, as with the instinctive fear that she might do the young lady a harm. But she quieted me with a glance I shall never forget – I confess I should like to have been able to paint *that* – and went for a moment to my model. She spoke to her softly, laying a hand upon her shoulder and bending over her; and as the girl, understanding, gratefully assented, she disposed her rough curls, with a few quick passes, in such a way as to make Miss Churm's head twice as charming. It was one of the most heroic personal services I have ever seen rendered. Then Mrs. Monarch turned away with a low sigh and, looking about her as if for something to do, stooped to the floor with a noble humility and picked up a dirty rag that had dropped out of my paint-box.

The Major meanwhile had also been looking for something to do and, wandering to the other end of the studio, saw before him my breakfast things, neglected, unremoved. "I say, can't I be useful *here?*" he called out to me with an irrepressible quaver. I assented with a laugh that I fear was awkward and for the next ten minutes, while I worked, I heard the light clatter of china and the tinkle of spoons and glass. Mrs. Monarch assisted her husband – they washed up my crockery, they put it away. They wandered off into my little scullery, and I afterwards found that they had cleaned my knives and that my slender stock of plate had an unprecedented surface. When it came over me, the latent eloquence of what they were doing, I confess that my drawing was blurred for a moment – the picture swam. They had accepted their failure, but they couldn't accept their fate. They had bowed their heads in bewilderment to the perverse and cruel law in virtue of which the real thing could be so much less precious than the unreal; but they didn't want to starve. If my servants were my models, my models might be my servants. They would reverse the parts – the others would sit for the ladies and gentlemen, and *they* would do the work. They would still be in the studio – it was an intense dumb appeal to me not to turn them out. "Take us on," they wanted to say – "we'll do *anything.*"

When all this hung before me the afflatus vanished – my pencil dropped from my hand. My sitting was spoiled and I got rid of my sitters, who were also evidently rather mystified and awestruck. Then, alone with the Major and his wife, I had a most uncomfortable moment, He put their prayer into a single sentence: "I say, you know – just let *us* do for you, can't you?" I couldn't – it was dreadful to see them emptying my slops; but I pretended I could, to oblige them, for about a week. Then I gave them a sum of money to go away; and I never saw them again. I obtained the remaining books, but my friend Hawley repeats that Major and Mrs. Monarch did me a permanent harm, got me into a second-rate trick. If it be true I am content to have paid the price – for the memory.

Sir Dominick Ferrand

Chapter I

"There are several objections to it, but I'll take it if you'll alter it," Mr. Locket's rather curt note had said; and there was no waste of words in the postscript in which he had added: "If you'll come in and see me, I'll show you what I mean." This communication had reached Jersey Villas by the first post, and Peter Baron had scarcely swallowed his leathery muffin before he got into motion to obey the editorial behest. He knew that such precipitation looked eager, and he had no desire to look eager – it was not in his interest; but how could he maintain a godlike calm, principled though he was in favor of it, the first time one of the great magazines had accepted, even with a cruel reservation, a specimen of his ardent young genius?

It was not till, like a child with a sea-shell at his ear, he began to be aware of the great roar of the "underground," that, in his third-class carriage, the cruelty of the reservation penetrated, with the taste of acrid smoke, to his inner sense. It was really degrading to be eager in the face of having to "alter." Peter Baron tried to figure to himself at that moment that he was not flying to betray the extremity of his need, but hurrying to fight for some of those passages of superior boldness which were exactly what the conductor of the "Promiscuous Review" would be sure to be down upon. He made believe – as if to the greasy fellow-passenger opposite – that he felt indignant; but he saw that to the small round eye of this still more downtrodden brother he represented selfish success. He would have liked to linger in the conception that he had been "approached" by the Promiscuous; but whatever might be thought in the office of that periodical of some of his flights of fancy, there was no want of vividness in his occasional suspicion that he passed there for a familiar bore. The only thing that was clearly flattering was the fact that the Promiscuous rarely published fiction. He should therefore be associated with a deviation from a solemn habit, and that would more than make up to him for a phrase in one of Mr. Locket's inexorable earlier notes, a phrase which still rankled, about his showing no symptom of the faculty really creative. "You don't seem able to keep a character together," this pitiless monitor had somewhere else remarked. Peter Baron, as he sat in his corner while the train stopped, considered, in the befogged gaslight, the bookstall standard of literature and asked himself whose character had fallen to pieces now. Tormenting indeed had always seemed to him such a fate as to have the creative head without the creative hand.

It should be mentioned, however, that before he started on his mission to Mr. Locket his attention had been briefly engaged by an incident occurring at Jersey Villas. On leaving the house (he lived at No. 3, the door of which stood open to a small front garden), he encountered the lady who, a week before, had taken possession of the rooms on the ground floor, the "parlors" of Mrs. Bundy's terminology. He had heard her, and from his window, two or three times, had even seen her pass in and out, and this observation had created in his mind a vague prejudice in her favor. Such a prejudice, it was true, had been subjected to a violent test; it had been fairly apparent that she had a light step, but it was still less to be overlooked that she had a cottage piano. She had furthermore a little boy and a very sweet voice, of which Peter Baron had caught the accent, not from her singing (for she only played), but from her gay admonitions to her child, whom she occasionally allowed to amuse himself – under restrictions very publicly enforced – in the tiny black patch which, as a forecourt to each house, was held, in the humble row, to be a feature. Jersey Villas stood in pairs, semi-detached, and Mrs. Ryves – such was the name under which the new lodger presented herself – had been admitted to the house as confessedly musical. Mrs. Bundy, the earnest proprietress of No. 3, who considered her "parlors" (they were a dozen feet square), even more attractive, if possible, than the second floor with which Baron had had to content himself – Mrs. Bundy, who reserved the drawing room for a casual dressmaking business, had threshed out the subject of the new lodger in advance with our young man, reminding him that her affection for his own person was a proof that, other things being equal, she positively preferred tenants who were clever.

This was the case with Mrs. Ryves; she had satisfied Mrs. Bundy that she was not a simple strummer. Mrs. Bundy admitted to Peter Baron that, for herself, she had a weakness for a pretty tune, and Peter could honestly reply that his ear was equally sensitive. Everything would depend on the "touch" of their inmate. Mrs. Ryves's piano would blight his existence if her hand should prove heavy or her selections vulgar; but if she played agreeable things and played them in an agreeable way she would render him rather a service while he smoked the pipe of "form." Mrs. Bundy, who wanted to let her rooms, guaranteed on the part of the stranger a first-class talent, and Mrs. Ryves, who evidently knew thoroughly what she was about, had not falsified this somewhat rash prediction. She never played in the morning, which was Baron's working-time, and he found himself listening with pleasure at other hours to her discreet and melancholy strains. He really knew little about music, and the only criticism he would have made of Mrs. Ryves's conception of it was that she seemed devoted to the dismal. It was not, however, that these strains were not pleasant to him; they floated up, on the contrary, as a sort of conscious response to some of his broodings and doubts. Harmony, therefore, would have reigned supreme had it not been for the singularly bad taste of No. 4. Mrs. Ryves's piano was on the free side of the house and was regarded by Mrs. Bundy as open to no objection but that of their own gentleman, who was so reasonable. As much, however, could not be said of the gentleman of No. 4, who had not even Mr. Baron's excuse of being "littery" (he kept a bull-terrier and had five hats – the street could count them), and whom, if you had listened to Mrs. Bundy, you would have supposed to be divided from the obnoxious instrument by walls and corridors, obstacles and intervals, of massive structure and fabulous extent. This gentleman had taken up an attitude which had now passed into the phase of correspondence and compromise; but it was the opinion of the immediate neighborhood that he had not a leg to stand upon, and on whatever subject the sentiment of Jersey Villas might have been vague, it was not so on the rights and the wrongs of landladies.

Mrs. Ryves's little boy was in the garden as Peter Baron issued from the house, and his mother appeared to have come out for a moment, bareheaded, to see that he was doing no harm. She was discussing with him the responsibility that he might incur by passing a piece of string round one of the iron palings and pretending he was in command of a "geegee"; but it happened that at the sight of the other lodger the child was seized with a finer perception of the drivable. He rushed at Baron with a flourish of the bridle, shouting, "Ou geegee!" in a manner productive of some refined embarrassment to his mother. Baron met his advance by mounting him on a shoulder and feigning to prance an instant, so that by the time this performance was over – it took but a few seconds – the young man felt introduced to Mrs. Ryves. Her smile struck him as charming, and such an impression shortens many steps. She said, "Oh, thank you – you mustn't let him worry you"; and then as, having put down the child and raised his hat, he was turning away, she added: "It's very good of you not to complain of my piano."

"I particularly enjoy it – you play beautifully," said Peter Baron.

"I have to play, you see – it's all I can do. But the people next door don't like it, though my room, you know, is not against their wall. Therefore I thank you for letting me tell them that you, in the house, don't find me a nuisance."

She looked gentle and bright as she spoke, and as the young man's eyes rested on her the tolerance for which she expressed herself indebted seemed to him the least indulgence she might count upon. But he only laughed and said "Oh, no, you're not a nuisance!" and felt more and more introduced.

The little boy, who was handsome, hereupon clamored for another ride, and she took him up herself, to moderate his transports. She stood a moment with the child in her arms, and he put his fingers exuberantly into her hair, so that while she smiled at Baron she slowly, permittingly shook her head to get rid of them.

"If they really make a fuss I'm afraid I shall have to go," she went on.

"Oh, don't go!" Baron broke out, with a sudden expressiveness which made his voice, as it fell upon his ear, strike him as the voice of another. She gave a vague exclamation and, nodding slightly but not unsociably, passed back into the house. She had made an impression which remained till the other party to the conversation reached the railway-station, when it was superseded by the thought of his prospective discussion with Mr. Locket. This was a proof of the intensity of that interest.

The aftertaste of the later conference was also intense for Peter Baron, who quitted his editor with his manuscript under his arm. He had had the question out with Mr. Locket, and he was in a flutter which ought to have been a sense of triumph and which indeed at first he succeeded in regarding in this light. Mr. Locket had had to admit that there was an idea in his story, and that was a tribute which Baron was in a position to make the most of. But there was also a scene which scandalized the editorial conscience and which the young man had promised to rewrite. The idea that Mr. Locket had been so good as to disengage depended for clearness mainly on this scene; so it was easy to see his objection was perverse. This inference was probably a part of the joy in which Peter Baron walked as he carried home a contribution it pleased him to classify as accepted. He walked to work off his excitement and to think in what manner he should reconstruct. He went some distance without settling that point, and then, as it began to worry him, he looked vaguely into shop windows for solutions and hints. Mr. Locket lived in the depths of Chelsea, in a little paneled, amiable house, and Baron took his way homeward along the King's Road. There was a new amusement for him, a fresher bustle, in a London walk in the morning; these were hours that he habitually spent at his table, in the awkward attitude engendered by the poor piece of furniture, one of the rickety features of Mrs. Bundy's second floor, which had to serve as his altar of literary sacrifice. If by exception he went out when the day was young he noticed that life seemed younger with it; there were livelier industries to profit by and shop-girls, often rosy, to look at; a different air was in the streets and a chaff of traffic for the observer of manners to catch. Above all, it was the time when poor Baron made his purchases, which were wholly of the wandering mind; his extravagances, for some mysterious reason, were all matutinal, and he had a foreknowledge that if ever he should ruin himself it would be well before noon. He felt lavish this morning, on the strength of what the Promiscuous would do for him; he had lost sight for the moment of what he should have to do for the Promiscuous. Before the old bookshops and print shops, the crowded panes of the curiosity-mongers and the desirable exhibitions of mahogany "done up," he used, by an innocent process, to commit luxurious follies. He refurnished Mrs. Bundy with a freedom that cost her nothing, and lost himself in pictures of a transfigured second floor.

On this particular occasion the King's Road proved almost unprecedentedly expensive, and indeed this occasion differed from most others in containing the germ of real danger. For once in a way he had a bad conscience – he felt himself tempted to pick his own pocket. He never saw a commodious writing-table, with elbow-room and drawers and a fair expanse of leather stamped neatly at the edge with gilt, without being freshly reminded of Mrs. Bundy's dilapidations. There were several such tables in the King's Road – they seemed indeed particularly numerous today. Peter Baron glanced at them all through the fronts of the shops, but there was one that detained him in supreme contemplation. There was a fine assurance about it which seemed a guarantee of masterpieces; but when at last he went in and, just to help himself on his way, asked the impossible price, the sum mentioned by the voluble vendor mocked at him even more than he had feared. It was far too expensive, as he hinted, and he was on the point of completing his comedy by a pensive retreat when the shopman bespoke his attention for another article of the same general character, which he described as remarkably cheap for what it was. It was an old piece, from a sale in the country, and it had been in stock some time; but it had got pushed out of sight in one of the upper rooms – they contained such a wilderness of treasures – and happened to have but just come to light. Peter suffered himself to be conducted into an interminable dusky rear, where he presently found himself bending over one of those square substantial desks of old mahogany, raised, with the aid of front legs, on a sort of retreating pedestal which is fitted with small drawers, contracted conveniences known immemorially to the knowing as davenports. This specimen had visibly seen service, but it had an old-time solidity and to Peter Baron it unexpectedly appealed.

He would have said in advance that such an article was exactly what he didn't want, but as the shopman pushed up a chair for him and he sat down with his elbows on the gentle slope of the large, firm lid, he felt that such a basis for literature would be half the battle. He raised the lid and looked lovingly into the deep interior; he sat ominously silent while his companion dropped the striking words: "Now that's an article I personally covet!" Then when the man mentioned the ridiculous price (they were literally giving it away), he reflected on the economy of having a literary altar on which one could really kindle a fire. A davenport was a compromise, but what was all life but a compromise? He could beat down the dealer, and at Mrs. Bundy's he had to write on an insincere card-table. After he had sat for a minute with his nose in the friendly desk he had a queer impression that it might tell him a secret or two – one of the secrets of form, one of the sacrificial mysteries – though no doubt its career had been literary only in the sense of its helping some old lady to write invitations to dull dinners. There was a strange, faint odor in the receptacle, as if fragrant, hallowed things had once been put away there. When he took his head out of it he said to the shopman: "I don't mind meeting you halfway." He had been told by knowing people that that was the right thing. He felt rather vulgar, but the davenport arrived that evening at Jersey Villas.

Chapter II

"I daresay it will be all right; he seems quiet now," said the poor lady of the "parlors" a few days later, in reference to their litigious neighbor and the precarious piano. The two lodgers had grown regularly acquainted, and the piano had had much to do with it. Just as this instrument served, with the gentleman at No. 4, as a theme for discussion, so between Peter Baron and the lady of the parlors it had become a basis of peculiar agreement, a topic, at any rate, of conversation frequently renewed. Mrs. Ryves was so prepossessing that Peter was sure that even if they had not had the piano he would have found something else to thresh out with her. Fortunately however they did have it, and he, at least, made the most of it, knowing more now about his new friend, who when, widowed and fatigued, she held her beautiful child in her arms, looked dimly like a modern Madonna. Mrs. Bundy, as a letter of furnished lodgings, was characterized in general by a familiar domestic severity in respect to picturesque young women, but she had the highest confidence in Mrs. Ryves. She was luminous about her being a lady, and a lady who could bring Mrs. Bundy back to a gratified recognition of one of those manifestations of mind for which she had an independent esteem. She was professional, but Jersey Villas could be proud of a profession that didn't happen to be the wrong one – they had seen something of that. Mrs. Ryves had a hundred a year (Baron wondered how Mrs. Bundy knew this; he thought it unlikely Mrs. Ryves had told her), and for the rest she depended on her lovely music. Baron judged that her music, even though lovely, was a frail dependence; it would hardly help to fill a concert-room, and he asked himself at first whether she played country-dances at children's parties or gave lessons to young ladies who studied above their station.

Very soon, indeed, he was sufficiently enlightened; it all went fast, for the little boy had been almost as great a help as the piano. Sidney haunted the doorstep of No. 3 he was eminently sociable, and had established independent relations with Peter, a frequent feature of which was an adventurous visit, upstairs, to picture books criticized for not being *all* geegees and walking sticks happily more conformable. The young man's window, too, looked out on their acquaintance; through a starched muslin curtain it kept his neighbor before him, made him almost more aware of her comings and goings than he felt he had a right to be. He was capable of a shyness of curiosity about her and of dumb little delicacies of consideration. She did give a few lessons; they were essentially local, and he ended by knowing more or less what she went out for and what she came in from. She had almost no visitors, only a decent old lady or two, and, every day, poor dingy Miss Teagle, who was also ancient and who came humbly enough to governess the infant of the parlors. Peter Baron's window had always, to his sense, looked out on a good deal of life, and one of the things it had most shown him was that there is nobody so bereft of joy as not to be able to command for twopence the services of somebody less joyous. Mrs. Ryves was a struggler (Baron scarcely liked to think of it), but she occupied a pinnacle for Miss Teagle, who had lived on – and from a noble nursery – into a period of diplomas and humiliation.

Mrs. Ryves sometimes went out, like Baron himself, with manuscripts under her arm, and, still more like Baron, she almost always came back with them. Her vain approaches were to the music-sellers; she tried to compose – to produce songs that would make a hit. A successful song was an income, she confided to Peter one of the first times he took Sidney, blasé and drowsy, back to his mother. It was not on one of these occasions, but once when he had come in on no better pretext than that of simply wanting to (she had after all virtually invited him), that she mentioned how only one song in a thousand was successful and that the terrible difficulty was in getting the right words. This rightness was just a vulgar "fluke" – there were lots of words really clever that were of no use at all. Peter said, laughing, that he supposed any words he should try to produce would be sure to be too clever; yet only three weeks after his first encounter with Mrs. Ryves he sat at his delightful davenport (well aware that he had duties more pressing), trying to string together rhymes idiotic enough to make his neighbor's fortune. He was satisfied of the fineness of her musical gift – it had the touching note. The touching note was in her person as well.

The davenport was delightful, after six months of its tottering predecessor, and such a re-enforcement to the young man's style was not impaired by his sense of something lawless in the way it had been gained. He had made the purchase in anticipation of the money he expected from Mr. Locket, but Mr. Locket's liberality was to depend on the ingenuity of his contributor, who now found himself confronted with the consequence of a frivolous optimism. The fruit of his labor presented, as he stared at it with his elbows on his desk, an aspect uncompromising and incorruptible. It seemed to look up at him reproachfully and to say, with its essential finish: "How could you promise anything so base; how could you pass your word to mutilate and dishonor me?" The alterations demanded by Mr. Locket were impossible; the concessions to the platitude of his conception of the public mind were degrading. The public mind! – as if the public *had* a mind, or any principle of perception more discoverable than the stare of huddled sheep! Peter Baron felt that it concerned him to determine if he were only not clever enough or if he were simply not abject enough to rewrite his story. He might in truth have had less pride if he had had more skill, and more discretion if he had had more practice. Humility, in the profession of letters, was half of practice, and resignation was half of success. Poor Peter actually flushed with pain as he recognized that this was not success, the production of gelid prose which his editor could do nothing with on the one side and he himself could do nothing with on the other. The truth about his luckless tale was now the more bitter from his having managed, for some days, to taste it as sweet.

As he sat there, baffled and somber, biting his pen and wondering what was meant by the "rewards" of literature, he generally ended by tossing away the composition deflowered by Mr. Locket and trying his hand at the sort of twaddle that Mrs. Ryves might be able to set to music. Success in these experiments wouldn't be a reward of literature, but it might very well become a labor of love. The experiments would be pleasant enough for him if they were pleasant for his inscrutable neighbor. That was the way he thought of her now, for he had learned enough about her, little by little, to guess how much there was still to learn. To spend his mornings over cheap rhymes for her was certainly to shirk the immediate question; but there were hours when he judged this question to be altogether too arduous, reflecting that he might quite as well perish by the sword as by famine. Besides, he did meet it obliquely when he considered that he shouldn't be an utter failure if he were to produce some songs to which Mrs. Ryves's accompaniments would give a circulation. He had not ventured to show her anything yet, but one morning, at a moment when her little boy was in his room, it seemed to him that, by an inspiration, he had arrived at the happy middle course (it was an art by itself), between sound and sense. If the sense was not confused it was because the sound was so familiar.

He had said to the child, to whom he had sacrificed barley-sugar (it had no attraction for his own lips, yet in these days there was always some of it about), he had confided to the small Sidney that if he would wait a little he should be entrusted with something nice to take down to his parent. Sidney had absorbing occupation and, while Peter copied off the song in a pretty hand, roamed, gurgling and sticky, about the room. In this manner he lurched like a little toper into the rear of the davenport, which stood a few steps out from the recess of the window, and, as he was fond of beating time to his intensest joys, began to bang on the surface of it with a paper-knife which at that spot had chanced to fall upon the floor. At the moment Sidney committed this violence his kind friend had happened to raise the lid of the desk and, with his head beneath it, was rummaging among a mass of papers for a proper envelope. "I say, I say, my boy!" he exclaimed, solicitous for the ancient glaze of his most cherished possession. Sidney paused an instant; then, while Peter still hunted for the envelope, he administered another, and this time a distinctly disobedient, rap. Peter heard it from within and was struck with its oddity of sound – so much so that, leaving the child for a moment under a demoralizing impression of impunity, he waited with quick curiosity for a repetition of the stroke. It came of course immediately, and then the young man, who had at the same instant found his envelope and ejaculated "Hallo, this thing has a false back!" jumped up and secured his visitor, whom with his left arm he held in durance on his knee while with his free hand he addressed the missive to Mrs. Ryves.

As Sidney was fond of errands he was easily got rid of, and after he had gone Baron stood a moment at the window chinking pennies and keys in pockets and wondering if the charming composer would think his song as good, or in other words as bad, as he thought it. His eyes as he turned away fell on the wooden back of the davenport, where, to his regret, the traces of Sidney's assault were visible in three or four ugly scratches. "Confound the little brute!" he exclaimed, feeling as if an altar had been desecrated. He was reminded, however, of the observation this outrage had led him to make, and, for further assurance, he knocked on the wood with his knuckle. It sounded from that position commonplace enough, but his suspicion was strongly confirmed when, again standing beside the desk, he put his head beneath the lifted lid and gave ear while with an extended arm he tapped sharply in the same place. The back was distinctly hollow; there was a space between the inner and the outer pieces (he could measure it), so wide that he was a fool not to have noticed it before. The depth of the receptacle from front to rear was so great that it could sacrifice a certain quantity of room without detection. The sacrifice could of course only be for a purpose, and the purpose could only be the creation of a secret compartment. Peter Baron was still boy enough to be thrilled by the idea of such a feature, the more so as every indication of it had been cleverly concealed. The people at the shop had never noticed it, else they would have called his attention to it as an enhancement of value. His legendary lore instructed him that where there was a hiding place there was always a hidden spring, and he pried and pressed and fumbled in an eager search for the sensitive spot. The article was really a wonder of neat construction; everything fitted with a closeness that completely saved appearances.

It took Baron some minutes to pursue his inquiry, during which he reflected that the people of the shop were not such fools after all. They had admitted moreover that they had accidentally neglected this relic of gentility – it had been overlooked in the multiplicity of their treasures. He now recalled that the man had wanted to polish it up before sending it home, and that, satisfied for his own part with its honorable appearance and averse in general to shiny furniture, he had in his impatience declined to wait for such an operation, so that the object had left the place for Jersey Villas, carrying presumably its secret with it, two or three hours after his visit. This secret it seemed indeed capable of keeping; there was an absurdity in being baffled, but Peter couldn't find the spring. He thumped and sounded, he listened and measured again; he inspected every joint and crevice, with the effect of becoming surer still of the existence of a chamber and of making up his mind that his davenport was a rarity. Not only was there a compartment between the two backs, but there was distinctly something *in* the compartment! Perhaps it was a lost manuscript – a nice, safe, old-fashioned story that Mr. Locket wouldn't object to. Peter returned to the charge, for it had occurred to him that he had perhaps not sufficiently visited the small drawers, of which, in two vertical rows, there were six in number, of different sizes, inserted sideways into that portion of the structure which formed part of the support of the desk. He took them out again and examined more minutely the condition of their sockets, with the happy result of discovering at last, in the place into which the third on the left-hand row was fitted, a small sliding panel. Behind the panel was a spring, like a flat button, which yielded with a click when he pressed it and which instantly produced a loosening of one of the pieces of the shelf forming the highest part of the davenport – pieces adjusted to each other with the most deceptive closeness.

This particular piece proved to be, in its turn, a sliding panel, which, when pushed, revealed the existence of a smaller receptacle, a narrow, oblong box, in the false back. Its capacity was limited, but if it couldn't hold many things it might hold precious ones. Baron, in presence of the ingenuity with which it had been dissimulated, immediately felt that, but for the odd chance of little Sidney Ryves's having hammered on the outside at the moment he himself happened to have his head in the desk, he might have remained for years without suspicion of it. This apparently would have been a loss, for he had been right in guessing that the chamber was not empty. It contained objects which, whether precious or not, had at any rate been worth somebody's hiding. These objects were a collection of small fiat parcels, of the shape of packets of letters, wrapped in white paper and neatly sealed. The seals, mechanically figured, bore the impress neither of arms nor of initials; the paper looked old – it had turned faintly sallow; the packets might have been there for ages. Baron counted them – there were nine in all, of different sizes; he turned them over and over, felt them curiously and snuffed in their vague, musty smell, which affected him with the melancholy of some smothered human accent. The little bundles were neither named nor numbered – there was not a word of writing on any of the covers; but they plainly contained old letters, sorted and matched according to dates or to authorship. They told some old, dead story – they were the ashes of fires burned out.

As Peter Baron held his discoveries successively in his hands he became conscious of a queer emotion which was not altogether elation and yet was still less pure pain. He had made a find, but it somehow added to his responsibility; he was in the presence of something interesting, but (in a manner he couldn't have defined) this circumstance suddenly constituted a danger. It was the perception of the danger, for instance, which caused to remain in abeyance any impulse he might have felt to break one of the seals. He looked at them all narrowly, but he was careful not to loosen them, and he wondered uncomfortably whether the contents of the secret compartment would be held in equity to be the property of the people in the King's Road. He had given money for the davenport, but had he given money for these buried papers? He paid by a growing consciousness that a nameless chill had stolen into the air the penalty, which he had many a time paid before, of being made of sensitive stuff. It was as if an occasion had insidiously arisen for a sacrifice – a sacrifice for the sake of a fine superstition, something like honor or kindness or justice, something indeed perhaps even finer still – a difficult deciphering of duty, an impossible tantalizing wisdom. Standing there before his ambiguous treasure and losing himself for the moment in the sense of a dawning complication, he was startled by a light, quick tap at the door of his sitting room. Instinctively, before answering, he listened an instant – he was in the attitude of a miser surprised while counting his hoard. Then he answered "One moment, please!" and slipped the little heap of packets into the biggest of the drawers of the davenport, which happened to be open. The aperture of the false back was still gaping, and he had not time to work back the spring. He hastily laid a big book over the place and then went and opened his door.

It offered him a sight nonetheless agreeable for being unexpected – the graceful and agitated figure of Mrs. Ryves. Her agitation was so visible that he thought at first that something dreadful had happened to her child – that she had rushed up to ask for help, to beg him to go for the doctor. Then he perceived that it was probably connected with the desperate verses he had transmitted to her a quarter of an hour before; for she had his open manuscript in one hand and was nervously pulling it about with the other. She looked frightened and pretty, and if, in invading the privacy of a fellow-lodger, she had been guilty of a departure from rigid custom, she was at least conscious of the enormity of the step and incapable of treating it with levity. The levity was for

Peter Baron, who endeavored, however, to clothe his familiarity with respect, pushing forward the seat of honor and repeating that he rejoiced in such a visit. The visitor came in, leaving the door ajar, and after a minute during which, to help her, he charged her with the purpose of telling him that he ought to be ashamed to send her down such rubbish, she recovered herself sufficiently to stammer out that his song was exactly what she had been looking for and that after reading it she had been seized with an extraordinary, irresistible impulse – that of thanking him for it in person and without delay.

"It was the impulse of a kind nature," he said, "and I can't tell you what pleasure you give me."

She declined to sit down, and evidently wished to appear to have come but for a few seconds. She looked confusedly at the place in which she found herself, and when her eyes met his own they struck him as anxious and appealing. She was evidently not thinking of his song, though she said three or four times over that it was beautiful. "Well, I only wanted you to know, and now I must go," she added; but on his hearthrug she lingered with such an odd helplessness that he felt almost sorry for her.

"Perhaps I can improve it if you find it doesn't go," said Baron. "I'm so delighted to do anything for you I can."

"There may be a word or two that might be changed," she answered, rather absently. "I shall have to think it over, to live with it a little. But I like it, and that's all I wanted to say."

"Charming of you. I'm not a bit busy," said Baron.

Again she looked at him with a troubled intensity, then suddenly she demanded: "Is there anything the matter with you?"

"The matter with me?"

"I mean like being ill or worried. I wondered if there might be; I had a sudden fancy; and that, I think, is really why I came up."

"There isn't, indeed; I'm all right. But your sudden fancies are inspirations."

"It's absurd. You must excuse me. Good-bye!" said Mrs. Ryves.

"What are the words you want changed?" Baron asked.

"I don't want any – if you're all right. Good-bye," his visitor repeated, fixing her eyes an instant on an object on his desk that had caught them. His own glanced in the same direction and he saw that in his hurry to shuffle away the packets found in the davenport he had overlooked one of them, which lay with its seals exposed. For an instant he felt found out, as if he had been concerned in something to be ashamed of, and it was only his quick second thought that told him how little the incident of which the packet was a sequel was an affair of Mrs. Ryves's.

Her conscious eyes came back to his as if they were sounding them, and suddenly this instinct of keeping his discovery to himself was succeeded by a really startled inference that, with the rarest alertness, she had guessed something and that her guess (it seemed almost supernatural), had been her real motive. Some secret sympathy had made her vibrate – had touched her with the knowledge that he had brought something to light. After an instant he saw that she also divined the very reflection he was then making, and this gave him a lively desire, a grateful, happy desire, to appear to have nothing to conceal. For herself, it determined her still more to put an end to her momentary visit. But before she had passed to the door he exclaimed: "All right? How can a fellow be anything else who has just had such a find?"

She paused at this, still looking earnest and asking: "What have you found?"

"Some ancient family papers, in a secret compartment of my writing-table." And he took up the packet he had left out, holding it before her eyes. "A lot of other things like that."

"What are they?" murmured Mrs. Ryves.

"I haven't the least idea. They're sealed."

"You haven't broken the seals?" She had come further back.

"I haven't had time; it only happened ten minutes ago."

"I knew it," said Mrs. Ryves, more gaily now.

"What did you know?"

"That you were in some predicament."

"You're extraordinary. I never heard of anything so miraculous; down two flights of stairs."

"Are you in a quandary?" the visitor asked.

"Yes, about giving them back." Peter Baron stood smiling at her and rapping his packet on the palm of his hand. "What do you advise?"

She herself smiled now, with her eyes on the sealed parcel. "Back to whom?"

"The man of whom I bought the table."

"Ah then, they're not from *your* family?"

"No indeed, the piece of furniture in which they were hidden is not an ancestral possession. I bought it at second hand – you see it's old – the other day in the King's Road. Obviously the man who sold it to me sold me more than he meant; he had no idea (from his own point of view it was stupid of him), that there was a hidden chamber or that mysterious documents were buried there. Ought I to go and tell him? It's rather a nice question."

"Are the papers of value?" Mrs. Ryves inquired.

"I haven't the least idea. But I can ascertain by breaking a seal."

"Don't!" said Mrs. Ryves, with much expression. She looked grave again.

"It's rather tantalizing – it's a bit of a problem," Baron went on, turning his packet over.

Mrs. Ryves hesitated. "Will you show me what you have in your hand?"

He gave her the packet, and she looked at it and held it for an instant to her nose. "It has a queer, charming old fragrance," he said.

"Charming? It's horrid." She handed him back the packet, saying again more emphatically "Don't!"

"Don't break a seal?"

"Don't give back the papers."

"Is it honest to keep them?"

"Certainly. They're yours as much as the people's of the shop. They were in the hidden chamber when the table came to the shop, and the people had every opportunity to find them out. They didn't – therefore let them take the consequences."

Peter Baron reflected, diverted by her intensity. She was pale, with eyes almost ardent. "The table had been in the place for years."

"That proves the things haven't been missed."

"Let me show you how they were concealed," he rejoined; and he exhibited the ingenious recess and the working of the curious spring. She was greatly interested, she grew excited and became familiar; she appealed to him again not to do anything so foolish as to give up the papers, the rest of which, in their little blank, impenetrable covers, he placed in a row before her. "They might be traced – their history, their ownership," he argued; to which she replied that this was exactly why he ought to be quiet. He declared that women had not the smallest sense of honor, and she retorted that at any rate they have other perceptions more delicate than those of men. He admitted that the papers might be rubbish, and she conceded that nothing was more probable; yet when he offered to settle the point off-hand she caught him by the wrist, acknowledging that, absurd as it was, she was nervous. Finally she put the whole thing on the ground of his just doing her a favor. She asked him to retain the papers, to be silent about them, simply because it would please her. That would be reason enough. Baron's acquaintance, his agreeable relations with her, advanced many steps in the treatment of this question; an element of friendly candor made its way into their discussion of it.

"I can't make out why it matters to you, one way or the other, nor why you should think it worth talking about," the young man reasoned.

"Neither can I. It's just a whim."

"Certainly, if it will give you any pleasure, I'll say nothing at the shop."

"That's charming of you, and I'm very grateful. I see now that this was why the spirit moved me to come up – to save them," Mrs. Ryves went on. She added, moving away, that now she had saved them she must really go.

"To save them for what, if I mayn't break the seals?" Baron asked.

"I don't know – for a generous sacrifice."

"Why should it be generous? What's at stake?" Peter demanded, leaning against the doorpost as she stood on the landing.

"I don't know what, but I feel as if something or other were in peril. Burn them up!" she exclaimed with shining eyes.

"Ah, you ask too much – I'm so curious about them!"

"Well, I won't ask more than I ought, and I'm much obliged to you for your promise to be quiet. I trust to your discretion. Good-bye."

"You ought to *reward* my discretion," said Baron, coming out to the landing.

She had partly descended the staircase and she stopped, leaning against the baluster and smiling up at him. "Surely you've had your reward in the honor of my visit."

"That's delightful as far as it goes. But what will you do for me if I burn the papers?"

Mrs. Ryves considered a moment. "Burn them first and you'll see!"

On this she went rapidly downstairs, and Baron, to whom the answer appeared inadequate and the proposition indeed in that form grossly unfair, returned to his room. The vivacity of her interest in a question in which she had discoverably nothing at stake mystified, amused and, in addition, irresistibly charmed him. She was delicate, imaginative, inflammable, quick to feel, quick to act. He didn't complain of it, it was the way he liked women to be;, but he was not impelled for the hour to commit the sealed packets to the flames. He dropped them again into their secret well, and after that he went out. He felt restless and excited; another day was lost for work – the dreadful job to be performed for Mr. Locket was still further off.

Chapter III

Ten days after Mrs. Ryves's visit he paid by appointment another call on the editor of the Promiscuous. He found him in the little wainscoted Chelsea house, which had to Peter's sense the smoky brownness of an old pipe bowl, surrounded with all the emblems of his office – a litter of papers, a hedge of encyclopedias, a photographic gallery of popular contributors – and he promised at first to consume very few of the moments for which so many claims competed. It was Mr. Locket himself however who presently made the interview spacious, gave it air after discovering that poor Baron had come to tell him something more interesting than that he couldn't after all patch up his tale. Peter had begun with this, had intimated respectfully that it was a case in which both practice and principle rebelled, and then, perceiving how little Mr. Locket was affected by his audacity, had felt weak and slightly silly, left with his heroism on his hands. He had armed himself for a struggle, but the Promiscuous didn't even protest, and there would have been nothing for him but to go away with the prospect of never coming again had he not chanced to say abruptly, irrelevantly, as he got up from his chair:

"Do you happen to be at all interested in Sir Dominick Ferrand?"

Mr. Locket, who had also got up, looked over his glasses. "The late Sir Dominick?"

"The only one; you know the family's extinct."

Mr. Locket shot his young friend another sharp glance, a silent retort to the glibness of this information. "Very extinct indeed. I'm afraid the subject today would scarcely be regarded as attractive."

"Are you very sure?" Baron asked.

Mr. Locket leaned forward a little, with his fingertips on his table, in the attitude of giving permission to retire. "I might consider the question in a special connection." He was silent a minute, in a way that relegated poor Peter to the general; but meeting the young man's eyes again he asked: "Are you – a – thinking of proposing an article upon him?"

"Not exactly proposing it – because I don't yet quite see my way; but the idea rather appeals to me."

Mr. Locket emitted the safe assertion that this eminent statesman had been a striking figure in his day; then he added: "Have you been studying him?"

"I've been dipping into him."

"I'm afraid he's scarcely a question of the hour," said Mr. Locket, shuffling papers together.

"I think I could make him one," Peter Baron declared.

Mr. Locket stared again; he was unable to repress an unattenuated "You?"

"I have some new material," said the young man, coloring a little. "That often freshens up an old story."

"It buries it sometimes. It's often only another tombstone."

"That depends upon what it is. However," Peter added, "the documents I speak of would be a crushing monument."

Mr. Locket, hesitating, shot another glance under his glasses. "Do you allude to – a – revelations?"

"Very curious ones."

Mr. Locket, still on his feet, had kept his body at the bowing angle; it was therefore easy for him after an instant to bend a little further and to sink into his chair with a movement of his hand toward the seat Baron had occupied. Baron resumed possession of this convenience, and the conversation took a fresh start on a basis which such an extension of privilege could render but little less humiliating to our young man. He had matured no plan of confiding his secret to Mr. Locket, and he had really come out to make him conscientiously that other announcement as to which it appeared that so much artistic agitation had been wasted. He had indeed during the past days – days of painful indecision – appealed in imagination to the editor of the Promiscuous, as he had appealed to other sources of comfort; but his scruples turned their face upon him from quarters high as well as low, and if on the one hand he had by no means made up his mind not to mention his strange knowledge, he had still more left to the determination of the moment the question of how he should introduce the subject. He was in fact too nervous to decide; he only felt that he needed for his peace of mind to communicate his discovery. He wanted an opinion, the impression of somebody else, and even in this intensely professional presence, five minutes after he had begun to tell his queer story, he felt relieved of half his burden. His story was very queer; he could take the measure of that himself as he spoke; but wouldn't this very circumstance qualify it for the Promiscuous?

"Of course the letters may be forgeries," said Mr. Locket at last.

"I've no doubt that's what many people will say."

"Have they been seen by any expert?"

"No indeed; they've been seen by nobody."

"Have you got any of them with you?"

"No; I felt nervous about bringing them out."

"That's a pity. I should have liked the testimony of my eyes."

"You may have it if you'll come to my rooms. If you don't care to do that without a further guarantee I'll copy you out some passages."

"Select a few of the worst!" Mr. Locket laughed. Over Baron's distressing information he had become quite human and genial. But he added in a moment more dryly: "You know they ought to be seen by an expert."

"That's exactly what I dread," said Peter.

"They'll be worth nothing to me if they're not."

Peter communed with his innermost spirit. "How much will they be worth to *me* if they *are*?"

Mr. Locket turned in his study-chair. "I should require to look at them before answering that question."

"I've been to the British museum – there are many of his letters there. I've obtained permission to see them, and I've compared everything carefully. I repudiate the possibility of forgery. No sign of genuineness is wanting; there are details, down to the very postmarks, that no forger could have invented. Besides, whose interest could it conceivably have been? A labor of unspeakable difficulty, and all for what advantage? There are so many letters, too – twenty-seven in all."

"Lord, what an ass!" Mr. Locket exclaimed.

"It will be one of the strangest post-mortem revelations of which history preserves the record."

Mr. Locket, grave now, worried with a paper-knife the crevice of a drawer. "It's very odd. But to be worth anything such documents should be subjected to a searching criticism – I mean of the historical kind."

"Certainly; that would be the task of the writer introducing them to the public."

Again Mr. Locket considered; then with a smile he looked up. "You had better give up original composition and take to buying old furniture."

"Do you mean because it will pay better?"

"For you, I should think, original composition couldn't pay worse. The creative faculty's so rare."

"I do feel tempted to turn my attention to real heroes," Peter replied.

"I'm bound to declare that Sir Dominick Ferrand was never one of mine. Flashy, crafty, second-rate – that's how I've always read him. It was never a secret, moreover, that his private life had its weak spots. He was a mere flash in the pan."

"He speaks to the people of this country," said Baron.

"He did; but his voice – the voice, I mean, of his prestige – is scarcely audible now."

"They're still proud of some of the things he did at the Foreign Office – the famous 'exchange' with Spain, in the Mediterranean, which took Europe so by surprise and by which she felt injured, especially when it became apparent how much we had the best of the bargain. Then the sudden, unexpected show of force by which he imposed on the United States our interpretation of that tiresome treaty – I could never make out what it was about. These were both matters that no one really cared a straw about, but he made everyone feel as if they cared; the nation rose to the way he played his trumps – it was uncommon. He was one of the few men we've had, in our period, who took Europe, or took America, by surprise, made them jump a bit; and the country liked his doing it – it was a pleasant change. The rest of the world considered that they knew in any case exactly what we would do, which was usually nothing at all. Say what you like, he's still a high name; partly also, no doubt, on account of other things his early success and early death, his political 'cheek' and wit; his very appearance – he certainly was handsome – and the possibilities (of future personal supremacy) which it was the fashion at the time, which it's the fashion still, to say had passed away with him. He had been twice at the Foreign Office; that alone was remarkable for a man dying at forty-four. What therefore will the country think when it learns he was venal?"

Peter Baron himself was not angry with Sir Dominick Ferrand, who had simply become to him (he had been "reading up" feverishly for a week) a very curious subject of psychological study; but he could easily put himself in the place of that portion of the public whose memory was long enough for their patriotism to receive a shock. It was some time fortunately since the conduct of public affairs had wanted for men of disinterested ability, but the extraordinary documents concealed (of all places in the world – it was as fantastic as a nightmare) in a "bargain" picked up at second-hand by an obscure scribbler, would be a calculable blow to the retrospective mind. Baron saw vividly that if these relics should be made public the scandal, the horror, the chatter would be immense. Immense would be also the contribution to truth, the rectification of history. He had felt for several days (and it was exactly what had made him so nervous) as if he held in his hand the key to public attention.

"There are too many things to explain," Mr. Locket went on, "and the singular provenance of your papers would count almost overwhelmingly against them even if the other objections were met. There would be a perfect and probably a very complicated pedigree to trace. How did they get into your davenport, as you call it, and how long had they been there? What hands secreted them? what hands had, so incredibly, clung to them and preserved them? Who are the persons mentioned in them? who are the correspondents, the parties to the nefarious transactions? You say the transactions appear to be of two distinct kinds – some of them connected with public business and others involving obscure personal relations."

"They all have this in common," said Peter Baron, "that they constitute evidence of uneasiness, in some instances of painful alarm, on the writer's part, in relation to exposure – the exposure in the one case, as I gather, of the fact that he had availed himself of official opportunities to promote enterprises (public works and that sort of thing) in which he had a pecuniary stake. The dread of the light in the other connection is evidently different, and these letters are the earliest in date. They are addressed to a woman, from whom he had evidently received money."

Mr. Locket wiped his glasses. "What woman?"

"I haven't the least idea. There are lots of questions I can't answer, of course; lots of identities I can't establish; lots of gaps I can't fill. But as to two points I'm clear, and they are the essential ones. In the first place the papers in my possession are genuine; in the second place they're compromising."

With this Peter Baron rose again, rather vexed with himself for having been led on to advertise his treasure (it was his interlocutor's perfectly natural skepticism that produced this effect), for he felt that he was putting himself in a false position. He detected in Mr. Locket's studied detachment the fermentation of impulses from which, unsuccessful as he was, he himself prayed to be delivered.

Mr. Locket remained seated; he watched Baron go across the room for his hat and umbrella. "Of course, the question would come up of whose property today such documents would legally he. There are heirs, descendants, executors to consider."

"In some degree perhaps; hut I've gone into that a little. Sir Dominick Ferrand had no children, and he left no brothers and no sisters. His wife survived him, but she died ten years ago. He can have had no heirs and no executors to speak of, for he left no property."

"That's to his honor and against your theory," said Mr. Locket.

"I *have* no theory. He left a largish mass of debt," Peter Baron added. At this Mr. Locket got up, while his visitor pursued: "So far as I can ascertain, though of course my inquiries have had to be very rapid and superficial, there is no one now living, directly or indirectly related to the personage in question, who would be likely to suffer from any steps in the direction of publicity. It happens to be a rare instance of a life that had, as it were, no loose ends. At least there are none perceptible at present."

"I see, I see," said Mr. Locket. "But I don't think I should care much for your article."

"What article?"

"The one you seem to wish to write, embodying this new matter."

"Oh, I don't wish to write it!" Peter exclaimed. And then he bade his host good-bye.

"Good-bye," said Mr. Locket. "Mind you, I don't say that I think there's nothing in it."

"You would think there was something in it if you were to see my documents."

"I should like to see the secret compartment,"

the caustic editor rejoined. "Copy me out some extracts."

"To what end, if there's no question of their being of use to you?"

"I don't say that – I might like the letters themselves."

"Themselves?"

"Not as the basis of a paper, but just to publish – for a sensation."

"They'd sell your number!" Baron laughed.

"I daresay I should like to look at them," Mr. Locket conceded after a moment. "When should I find you at home?"

"Don't come," said the young man. "I make you no offer."

"I might make *you* one," the editor hinted. "Don't trouble yourself; I shall probably destroy them." With this Peter Baron took his departure, waiting however just afterwards, in the street near the house, as if he had been looking out for a stray hansom, to which he would not have signaled had it appeared. He thought Mr. Locket might hurry after him, but Mr. Locket seemed to have other things to do, and Peter Baron returned on foot to Jersey Villas.

Chapter IV

On the evening that succeeded this apparently pointless encounter he had an interview more conclusive with Mrs. Bundy, for whose shrewd and philosophic view of life he had several times expressed, even to the good woman herself, a considerable relish. The situation at Jersey Villas (Mrs. Ryves had suddenly flown off to Dover) was such as to create in him a desire for moral support, and there was a kind of domestic determination in Mrs. Bundy which seemed, in general, to advertise it. He had asked for her on coming in, but had been told she was absent for the hour; upon which he had addressed himself mechanically to the task of doing up his dishonored manuscript – the ingenious fiction about which Mr. Locket had been so stupid – for further adventures and not improbable defeats. He passed a restless, ineffective afternoon, asking himself if his genius were a horrid delusion, looking out of his window for something that didn't happen, something that seemed now to be the advent of a persuasive Mr. Locket and now the return, from an absence more disappointing even than Mrs. Bundy's, of his interesting neighbor of the parlors. He was so nervous and so depressed that he was unable even to fix his mind on the composition of the note with which, on its next peregrination, it was necessary that his manuscript should be accompanied. He was too nervous to eat, and he forgot even to dine; he forgot to light his candles, he let his fire go out, and it was in the melancholy chill of the late dusk that Mrs. Bundy, arriving at last with his lamp, found him extended moodily upon his sofa. She had been informed that he wished to speak to her, and as she placed on the malodorous luminary an oily shade of green pasteboard she expressed the friendly hope that there was nothing wrong with his 'ealth.

The young man rose from his couch, pulling himself together sufficiently to reply that his health was well enough but that his spirits were down in his hoots. He had a strong disposition to "draw" his landlady on the subject of Mrs. Ryves, as well as a vivid conviction that she constituted a theme as to which Mrs. Bundy would require little pressure to tell him even more than she knew. At the same time he hated to appear to pry into the secrets of his absent friend; to discuss her with their bustling hostess resembled too much for his taste a gossip with a tattling servant about an unconscious employer. He left out of account however Mrs. Bundy's knowledge of the human heart, for it was this fine principle that broke down the barriers after he had reflected reassuringly that it was not meddling with Mrs. Ryves's affairs to try and find out if she struck such an observer as happy. Crudely, abruptly, even a little blushingly, he put the direct question to Mrs. Bundy, and this led tolerably straight to another question, which, on his spirit, sat equally heavy (they were indeed but different phases of the same), and which the good woman answered with expression when she ejaculated: "Think it a liberty for you to run down for a few hours? If she do, my dear sir, just send her to me to talk to!" As regards happiness indeed she warned Baron against imposing too high a standard on a young thing who had been through so much, and before he knew it he found himself, without the responsibility of choice, in submissive receipt of Mrs. Bundy's version of this experience. It was an interesting picture, though it had its infirmities, one of them congenital and consisting of the fact that it had sprung essentially from the virginal brain of Miss Teagle. Amplified, edited, embellished by the richer genius of Mrs. Bundy, who had incorporated with it and now liberally introduced copious interleavings of Miss Teagle's own romance, it gave Peter Baron much food for meditation, at the same time that it only half relieved his curiosity about the causes of the charming woman's underlying strangeness. He sounded this note experimentally in Mrs. Bundy's ear, but it was easy to see that it didn't reverberate in her fancy. She had no idea of the picture it would have been natural for him to desire that Mrs. Ryves should present to him, and she was therefore unable to estimate the points in respect to which his actual impression was irritating. She had indeed no adequate conception of the intellectual requirements of a young man in love. She couldn't tell him why their faultless friend was so isolated, so unrelated, so nervously, shrinkingly proud. On the other hand she could tell him (he knew it already) that she had passed many years of her life in the acquisition of accomplishments at a seat of learning no less remote than Boulogne, and that Miss Teagle had been intimately acquainted with the late Mr. Everard Ryves, who was a "most rising" young man in the city, not making any year less than his clear twelve hundred. "Now that he isn't there to make them, his mourning widow can't live as she had then, can she?" Mrs. Bundy asked.

Baron was not prepared to say that she could, but he thought of another way she might live as he sat, the next day, in the train which rattled him down to Dover. The place, as he approached it, seemed bright and breezy to him; his roamings had been neither far enough nor frequent enough to make the cockneyfied coast insipid. Mrs. Bundy had of course given him the address he needed, and on emerging from the station he was on the point of asking what direction he should take. His attention however at this moment was drawn away by the bustle of the departing boat. He had been long enough shut up in London to be conscious of refreshment in the mere act of turning his face to Paris. He wandered off to the pier in company with happier tourists and, leaning on a rail, watched enviously the preparation, the agitation of foreign travel. It was for some minutes a foretaste of adventure; but, ah, when was he to have the very draught? He turned away as he dropped this interrogative sigh, and in doing so perceived that in another part of the pier two ladies and a little boy were gathered with something of the same wistfulness. The little boy indeed happened to look round for a moment, upon which, with the keenness of the predatory age, he recognized in our young man a source of pleasures from which he lately had been weaned. He bounded forward with irrepressible cries of "Geegee!" and Peter lifted him aloft for an embrace. On putting him down the pilgrim from Jersey Villas stood confronted with a sensibly severe Miss Teagle, who had followed her little charge. "What's the matter with the old woman?" he asked himself as he offered her a hand which she treated as the merest detail. Whatever it was, it was (and very properly, on the part of a loyal suivante) the same complaint as that of her employer, to whom, from a distance, for Mrs. Ryves had not advanced an inch, he flourished his hat as she stood looking at him with a face that he imagined rather white. Mrs. Ryves's response to this salutation was to shift her position in such a manner as to appear again absorbed in the Calais boat. Peter Baron, however, kept hold of the child, whom Miss Teagle artfully endeavored to wrest from him – a policy in which he was aided by Sidney's own rough but instinctive loyalty; and he was thankful for the happy effect of being dragged by his jubilant friend in the very direction in which he had tended for so many hours. Mrs. Ryves turned once more as he came near, and then, from the sweet, strained smile with which she asked him if he were on his way to France, he saw that if she had been angry at his having followed her she had quickly got over it.

"No, I'm not crossing; but it came over me that you might be, and that's why I hurried down – to catch you before you were off."

"Oh, we can't go – more's the pity; but why, if we could," Mrs. Ryves inquired, "should you wish to prevent it?"

"Because I've something to ask you first, something that may take some time." He saw now that her embarrassment had really not been resentful; it had been nervous, tremulous, as the emotion of an unexpected pleasure might have been. "That's really why I determined last night, without asking your leave first to pay you this little visit – that and the intense desire for another bout of horse-play with Sidney. Oh, I've come to see you," Peter Baron went on, "and I won't make any secret of the fact that I expect you to resign yourself gracefully to the trial and give me all your time. The day's lovely, and I'm ready to declare that the place is as good as the day. Let me drink deep of these things, drain the cup like a man who hasn't been out of London for months and months. Let me walk with you and talk with you and lunch with you – I go back this afternoon. Give me all your hours in short, so that they may live in my memory as one of the sweetest occasions of life."

The emission of steam from the French packet made such an uproar that Baron could breathe his passion into the young woman's ear without scandalizing the spectators; and the charm which little by little it scattered over his fleeting visit proved indeed to be the collective influence of the conditions he had put into words. "What is it you wish to ask me?" Mrs. Ryves demanded, as they stood there together; to which he replied that he would tell her all about it if she would send Miss Teagle off with Sidney. Miss Teagle, who was always anticipating her cue, had already begun ostentatiously to gaze at the distant shores of France and was easily enough induced to take an earlier start home and rise to the responsibility of stopping on her way to contend with the butcher. She had however to retire without Sidney, who clung to his recovered prey, so that the rest of the episode was seasoned, to Baron's sense, by the importunate twitch of the child's little, plump, cool hand. The friends wandered together with a conjugal air and Sidney not between them, hanging wistfully, first, over the lengthened picture of the Calais boat, till they could look after it, as it moved rumbling away, in a spell of silence which seemed to confess – especially when, a moment later, their eyes met – that it produced the same fond fancy in each. The presence of the boy moreover was no hindrance to their talking in a manner that they made believe was very frank. Peter Baron presently told his companion what it was he had taken a journey to ask, and he had time afterwards to get over his discomfiture at her appearance of having fancied it might be something greater. She seemed disappointed (but she was forgiving) on learning from him that he had only wished to know if she judged ferociously his not having complied with her request to respect certain seals.

"How ferociously do you suspect me of having judged it?" she inquired.

"Why, to the extent of leaving the house the next moment."

They were still lingering on the great granite pier when he touched on this matter, and she sat down at the end while the breeze, warmed by the sunshine, ruffled the purple sea. She colored a little and looked troubled, and after an instant she repeated interrogatively: "The next moment?"

"As soon as I told you what I had done. I was scrupulous about this, you will remember; I went straight downstairs to confess to you. You turned away from me, saying nothing; I couldn't imagine – as I vow I can't imagine now – why such a matter should appear so closely to touch you. I went out on some business and when I returned you had quitted the house. It had all the look of my having offended you, of your wishing to get away from me. You didn't even give me time to tell you how it was that, in spite of your advice, I determined to see for myself what my discovery represented. You must do me justice and hear what determined me."

Mrs. Ryves got up from her scat and asked him, as a particular favor, not to allude again to his discovery. It was no concern of hers at all, and she had no warrant for prying into his secrets. She was very sorry to have been for a moment so absurd as to appear to do so, and she humbly begged his pardon for her meddling. Saying this she walked on with a charming color in her cheek, while he laughed out, though he was really bewildered, at the endless capriciousness of women. Fortunately the incident didn't spoil the hour, in which there were other sources of satisfaction, and they took their course to her lodgings with such pleasant little pauses and excursions by the way as permitted her to show him the objects of interest at Dover. She let him stop at a wine-merchant's and buy a bottle for luncheon, of which, in its order, they partook, together with a pudding invented by Miss Teagle, which, as they hypocritically swallowed it, made them look at each other in an intimacy of indulgence. They came out again and, while Sidney grubbed in the gravel of the shore, sat selfishly on the Parade, to the disappointment of Miss Teagle, who had fixed her hopes on a fly and a ladylike visit to the castle. Baron had his eye on his watch – he had to think of his train and the dismal return and many other melancholy things; but the sea in the afternoon light was a more appealing picture; the wind had gone down, the Channel was crowded, the sails of the ships were white in the purple distance. The young man had asked his companion (he had asked her before) when she was to come back to Jersey Villas, and she had said that she should probably stay at Dover another week. It was dreadfully expensive, but it was doing the child all the good in the world, and if Miss Teagle could go up for some things she should probably be able to manage an extension. Earlier in the day she had said that she perhaps wouldn't return to Jersey Villas at all, or only return to wind up her connection with Mrs. Bundy. At another moment she had spoken of an early date, an immediate reoccupation of the wonderful parlors. Baron saw that she had no plan, no real reasons, that she was vague and, in secret, worried and nervous, waiting for something that didn't depend on herself. A silence of several minutes had fallen upon them while they watched the shining sails; to which Mrs. Ryves put an end by exclaiming abruptly, but without completing her sentence: "Oh, if you had come to tell me you had destroyed them –"

"Those terrible papers? I like the way you talk about 'destroying!' You don't even know what they are."

"I don't want to know; they put me into a state."

"What sort of a state?"

"I don't know; they haunt me."

"They haunted me; that was why, early one morning, suddenly, I couldn't keep my hands off them. I had told you I wouldn't touch them. I had deferred to your whim, your superstition (what is it?) but at last they got the better of me. I had lain awake all night threshing about, itching with curiosity. It made me ill; my own nerves (as I may say) were irritated, my capacity to work was gone. It had come over me in the small hours in the shape of an obsession, a fixed idea, that there was nothing in the ridiculous relics and that my exaggerated scruples were making a fool of me. It was ten to one they were rubbish, they were vain, they were empty; that they had been even a practical joke on the part of some weak-minded gentleman of leisure, the former possessor of the confounded davenport. The longer I hovered about them with such precautions the longer I was taken in, and the sooner I exposed their insignificance the sooner I should get back to my usual occupations. This conviction made my hand so uncontrollable that that morning before breakfast I broke one of the seals. It took me but a few minutes to perceive that the contents were not rubbish; the little bundle contained old letters – very curious old letters."

"I know – I know; 'private and confidential.' So you broke the other seals?" Mrs. Ryves looked at him with the strange apprehension he had seen in her eyes when she appeared at his door the moment after his discovery.

"You know, of course, because I told you an hour later, though you would let me tell you very little."

Baron, as he met this queer gaze, smiled hard at her to prevent her guessing that he smarted with the fine reproach conveyed in the tone of her last words; but she appeared able to guess everything, for she reminded him that she had not had to wait that morning till he came downstairs to know what had happened above, but had shown him at the moment how she had been conscious of it an hour before, had passed on her side the same tormented night as he, and had had to exert extraordinary self-command not to rush up to his rooms while the study of the open packets was going on. "You're so sensitively organized and you've such mysterious powers that you re uncanny," Baron declared.

"I feel what takes place at a distance; that's all."

"One would think somebody you liked was in danger."

"I told you that that was what was present to me the day I came up to see you."

"Oh, but you don't like me so much as that," Baron argued, laughing.

She hesitated. "No, I don't know that I do."

"It must be for someone else – the other person concerned. The other day, however, you wouldn't let me tell you that person's name."

Mrs. Ryves, at this, rose quickly. "I don't want to know it; it's none of my business."

"No, fortunately, I don't think it is," Baron rejoined, walking with her along the Parade. She had Sidney by the hand now, and the young man was on the other side of her. They moved toward the station – she had offered to go part of the way. "But with your miraculous gift it's a wonder you haven't divined."

"I only divine what I want," said Mrs. Ryves.

"That's very convenient!" exclaimed Peter, to whom Sidney had presently come round again. "Only, being thus in the dark, it's difficult to see your motive for wishing the papers destroyed."

Mrs. Ryves meditated, looking fixedly at the ground. "I thought you might do it to oblige me."

"Does it strike you that such an expectation, formed in such conditions, is reasonable?"

Mrs. Ryves stopped short, and this time she turned on him the clouded clearness of her eyes. "What do you mean to do with them?"

It was Peter Baron's turn to meditate, which he did, on the empty asphalt of the Parade (the "season," at Dover, was not yet), where their shadows were long in the afternoon light. He was under such a charm as he had never known, and he wanted immensely to be able to reply: "I'll do anything you like if you'll love me." These words, however, would have represented a responsibility and have constituted what was vulgarly termed an offer. An offer of what? he quickly asked himself here, as he had already asked himself after making in spirit other awkward dashes in the same direction – of what but his poverty, his obscurity, his attempts that had come to nothing, his abilities for which there was nothing to show? Mrs. Ryves was not exactly a success, but she was a greater success than Peter Baron. Poor as he was he hated the sordid (he knew she didn't love it), and he felt small for talking of marriage. Therefore he didn't put the question in the words it would have pleased him most to hear himself utter, but he compromised, with an angry young pang, and said to her: "What will you do for me if I put an end to them?"

She shook her head sadly – it was always her prettiest movement. "I can promise nothing – oh, no, I can't promise! We must part now," she added. "You'll miss your train."

He looked at his watch, taking the hand she held out to him. She drew it away quickly, and nothing then was left him, before hurrying to the station, but to catch up Sidney and squeeze him till he uttered a little shriek. On the way back to town the situation struck him as grotesque.

Chapter V

It tormented him so the next morning that after threshing it out a little further he felt he had something of a grievance. Mrs. Ryves's intervention had made him acutely uncomfortable, for she had taken the attitude of exerting pressure without, it appeared, recognizing on his part an equal right. She had imposed herself as an influence, yet she held herself aloof as a participant; there were things she looked to him to do for her, yet she could tell him of no good that would come to him from the doing. She should either have had less to say or have been willing to say more, and he asked himself why he should be the sport of her moods and her mysteries. He perceived her knack of punctual interference to be striking, but it was just this apparent infallibility that he resented. Why didn't she set up at once as a professional clairvoyant and eke out her little income more successfully? In purely private life such a gift was disconcerting; her divinations, her evasions disturbed at any rate his own tranquility.

What disturbed it still further was that he received early in the day a visit from Mr. Locket, who, leaving him under no illusion as to the grounds of such an honor, remarked as soon as he had got into the room or rather while he still panted on the second flight and the smudged little slavey held open Baron's door, that he had taken up his young friend's invitation to look at Sir Dominick Ferrand's letters for himself. Peter drew them forth with a promptitude intended to show that he recognized the commercial character of the call and without attenuating the inconsequence of this departure from the last determination he had expressed to Mr. Locket. He showed his visitor the davenport and the hidden recess, and he smoked a cigarette, humming softly, with a sense of unwonted advantage and triumph, while the cautious editor sat silent and handled the papers. For all his caution Mr. Locket was unable to keep a warmer light out of his judicial eye as he said to Baron at last with sociable brevity – a tone that took many things for granted: "I'll take them home with me – they require much attention."

The young man looked at him a moment. "Do you think they're genuine?" He didn't mean to be mocking, he meant not to be; but the words sounded so to his own ear, and he could see that they produced that effect on Mr. Locket.

"I can't in the least determine. I shall have to go into them at my leisure, and that's why I ask you to lend them to me."

He had shuffled the papers together with a movement charged, while he spoke, with the air of being preliminary to that of thrusting them into a little black bag which he had brought with him and which, resting on the shelf of the davenport, struck Peter, who viewed it askance, as an object darkly editorial. It made our young man, somehow, suddenly apprehensive; the advantage of which he had just been conscious was about to be transferred by a quiet process of legerdemain to a person who already had advantages enough. Baron, in short, felt a deep pang of anxiety; he couldn't have said why. Mr. Locket took decidedly too many things for granted, and the explorer of Sir Dominick Ferrand's irregularities remembered afresh how clear he had been after all about his indisposition to traffic in them. He asked his visitor to what end he wished to remove the letters, since on the one hand there was no question now of the article in the Promiscuous which was to reveal their existence, and on the other he himself, as their owner, had a thousand insurmountable scruples about putting them into circulation.

Mr. Locket looked over his spectacles as over the battlements of a fortress. "I'm not thinking of the end – I'm thinking of the beginning. A few glances have assured me that such documents ought to be submitted to some competent eye."

"Oh, you mustn't show them to anyone!" Baron exclaimed.

"You may think me presumptuous, but the eye that I venture to allude to in those terms –"

"Is the eye now fixed so terribly on *me?*" Peter laughingly interrupted. "Oh, it would be interesting, I confess, to know how they strike a man of your acuteness!" It had occurred to him that by such a concession he might endear himself to a literary umpire hitherto implacable. There would be no question of his publishing Sir Dominick Ferrand, but he might, in due acknowledgment of services rendered, form the habit of publishing Peter Baron. "How long would it be your idea to retain them?" he inquired, in a manner which, he immediately became aware, was what incited Mr. Locket to begin stuffing the papers into his bag. With this perception he came quickly closer and, laying his hand on the gaping receptacle, lightly drew its two lips together. In this way the two men stood for a few seconds, touching, almost in the attitude of combat, looking hard into each other's eyes.

The tension was quickly relieved however by the surprised flush which mantled on Mr. Locket's brow. He fell back a few steps with an injured dignity that might have been a protest against physical violence. "Really, my dear young sir, your attitude is tantamount to an accusation of intended bad faith. Do you think I want to steal the confounded things?" In reply to such a challenge Peter could only hastily declare that he was guilty of no discourteous suspicion – he only wanted a limit named, a pledge of every precaution against accident. Mr. Locket admitted the justice of the demand, assured him he would restore the property within three days, and completed, with Peter's assistance, his little arrangements for removing it discreetly. When he was ready, his treacherous reticule distended with its treasures, he gave a lingering look at the inscrutable davenport. "It's how they ever got into that thing that puzzles one's brain!"

"There was some concatenation of circumstances that would doubtless seem natural enough if it were explained, but that one would have to remount the stream of time to ascertain. To one course I have definitely made up my mind: not to make any statement or any inquiry at the shop. I simply accept the mystery," said Peter, rather grandly.

"That would be thought a cheap escape if you were to put it into a story," Mr. Locket smiled.

"Yes, I shouldn't offer the story to *you.* I shall be impatient till I see my papers again," the young man called out, as his visitor hurried downstairs.

That evening, by the last delivery, he received, under the Dover postmark, a letter that was not from Miss Teagle. It was a slightly confused but altogether friendly note, written that morning after breakfast, the ostensible purpose of which was to thank him for the amiability of his visit, to express regret at any appearance the writer might have had of meddling with what didn't concern her, and to let him know that the evening before, after he had left her, she had in a moment of inspiration got hold of the tail of a really musical idea – a perfect accompaniment for the song he had so kindly given her. She had scrawled, as a specimen, a few bars at the end of her note, mystic, mocking musical signs which had no sense for her correspondent. The whole letter testified to a restless but rather pointless desire to remain in communication with him. In answering her, however, which he did that night before going to bed, it was on this bright possibility of their collaboration, its advantages for the future of each of them, that Baron principally expatiated. He spoke of this future with an eloquence of which he would have defended the sincerity, and drew of it a picture extravagantly rich. The next morning, as he was about to settle himself to tasks for some time terribly neglected, with a sense that after all it was rather a relief not to be sitting so close to Sir Dominick Ferrand, who had become dreadfully distracting; at the very moment at which he habitually addressed his preliminary invocation to the muse, he was agitated by the arrival of a telegram which proved to be an urgent request from Mr. Locket that he would immediately come down and see him. This represented, for poor Baron, whose funds were very low, another morning sacrificed, but somehow it didn't even occur to him that he might impose his own time upon the editor of the Promiscuous, the keeper of the keys of renown. He had some of the plasticity of the raw contributor. He gave the muse another holiday, feeling she was really ashamed to take it, and in course of time found himself in Mr. Locket's own chair at Mr. Locket's own table – so much nobler an expanse than the slippery slope of the davenport – considering with quick intensity, in the white flash of certain words just brought out by his host, the quantity of happiness, of emancipation that might reside in a hundred pounds.

Yes, that was what it meant: Mr. Locket, in the twenty-four hours, had discovered so much in Sir Dominick's literary remains that his visitor found him primed with an offer. A hundred pounds would be paid him that day, that minute, and no questions would be either asked or answered. "I take all the risks, I take all the risks," the editor of the Promiscuous repeated. The letters were out on the table, Mr. Locket was on the hearthrug, like an orator on a platform, and Peter, under the influence of his sudden ultimatum, had dropped, rather weakly, into the seat which happened to be nearest and which, as he became conscious it moved on a pivot, he whirled round so as to enable himself to look at his tempter with an eye intended to be cold. What surprised him most was to find Mr. Locket taking exactly the line about the expediency of publication which he would have expected Mr. Locket not to take. "Hush it all up; a barren scandal, an offence that can't be remedied, is the thing in the world that least justifies an airing –" some such line as that was the line he would have thought natural to a man whose life was spent in weighing questions of propriety and who had only the other day objected, in the light of this virtue, to a work of the most disinterested art. But the author of that incorruptible masterpiece had put his finger on the place in saying to his interlocutor on the occasion of his last visit that, if given to the world in the pages of the Promiscuous, Sir Dominick's aberrations would sell the edition. It was not necessary for Mr. Locket to reiterate to his young friend his phrase about their making a sensation. If he wished to purchase the "rights," as theatrical people said, it was not to protect a celebrated name or to lock them up in a cupboard. That formula of Baron's covered all the ground, and one edition was a low estimate of the probable performance of the magazine.

Peter left the letters behind him and, on withdrawing from the editorial presence, took a long walk on the Embankment. His impressions were at war with each other – he was flurried by possibilities of which he yet denied the existence. He had consented to trust Mr. Locket with the papers a day or two longer, till he should have thought out the terms on which he might – in the event of certain occurrences – be induced to dispose of them. A hundred pounds were not this gentleman's last word, nor perhaps was mere unreasoning intractability Peter's own. He sighed as he took no note of the pictures made by barges – sighed because it all might mean money. He needed money bitterly; he owed it in disquieting quarters. Mr. Locket had put it before him that he had a high responsibility – that he might vindicate the disfigured truth, contribute a chapter to the history of England. "You haven't a right to suppress such momentous facts," the hungry little editor had declared, thinking how the series (he would spread it into three numbers) would be the talk of the town. If Peter had money he might treat himself to ardor, to bliss. Mr. Locket had said, no doubt justly enough, that there were ever so many questions one would have to meet should one venture to play so daring a game. These questions, embarrassments, dangers – the danger, for instance, of the cropping-up of some lurking litigious relative – he would take over unreservedly and bear the brunt of dealing with. It was to be remembered that the papers were discredited, vitiated by their childish pedigree; such a preposterous origin, suggesting, as he had hinted before, the feeble ingenuity of a third-rate novelist, was a thing he should have to place himself at the positive disadvantage of being silent about. He would rather give no account of the matter at all than expose himself to the ridicule that such a story would infallibly excite. Couldn't one see them in advance, the clever, taunting things the daily and weekly papers would say? Peter Baron had his guileless side, but he felt, as he worried with a stick that betrayed him the granite parapets of the Thames, that he was not such a fool as not to know how Mr. Locket would "work" the mystery of his marvelous find. Nothing could help it on better with the public than the impenetrability of the secret attached to it. If Mr. Locket should only be able to kick up dust enough over the circumstances that had guided his hand his fortune would literally be made. Peter thought a hundred pounds a low bid, yet he wondered how the Promiscuous could bring itself to offer such a sum – so large it loomed in the light of literary remuneration as hitherto revealed to our young man. The explanation of this anomaly was of course that the editor shrewdly saw a dozen ways of getting his money back. There would be in the "sensation," at a later stage, the making of a book in large type – the book of the hour; and the profits of this scandalous volume or, if one preferred the name, this reconstruction, before an impartial posterity, of a great historical humbug, the sum "down," in other words, that any lively publisher would give for it, figured vividly in Mr. Locket's calculations. It was therefore altogether an opportunity of dealing at first hand with the lively publisher that Peter was invited to forego. Peter gave a masterful laugh, rejoicing in his heart that, on the spot, in the repaire he had lately quitted, he had not been tempted by a figure that would have approximately represented the value of his property. It was a good job, he mentally added as he turned his face homeward, that there was so little likelihood of his having to struggle with that particular pressure.

Chapter VI

When, half an hour later, he approached Jersey Villas, he noticed that the house-door was open; then, as he reached the gate, saw it make a frame for an unexpected presence. Mrs. Ryves, in her bonnet and jacket, looked out from it as if she were expecting something – as if she had been passing to and fro to watch. Yet when he had expressed to her that it was a delightful welcome she replied that she had only thought there might possibly be a cab in sight. He offered to go and look for one, upon which it appeared that after all she was not, as yet at least, in need. He went back with her into her sitting room, where she let him know that within a couple of days she had seen clearer what was best; she had determined to quit Jersey Villas and had come up to take away her things, which she had just been packing and getting together.

"I wrote you last night a charming letter in answer to yours," Baron said. "You didn't mention in yours that you were coming up."

"It wasn't your answer that brought me. It hadn't arrived when I came away."

"You'll see when you get back that my letter is charming."

"I daresay." Baron had observed that the room was not, as she had intimated, in confusion – Mrs. Ryves's preparations for departure were not striking. She saw him look round and, standing in front of the fireless grate with her hands behind her, she suddenly asked: "Where have you come from now?"

"From an interview with a literary friend."

"What are you concocting between you?"

"Nothing at all. We've fallen out – we don't agree."

"Is he a publisher?"

"He's an editor."

"Well, I'm glad you don't agree. I don't know what he wants, but, whatever it is, don't do it."

"He must do what *I* want!" said Baron.

"And what's that?"

"Oh, I'll tell you when he has done it!" Baron begged her to let him hear the "musical idea" she had mentioned in her letter; on which she took off her hat and jacket and, seating herself at her piano, gave him, with a sentiment of which the very first notes thrilled him, the accompaniment of his song. She phrased the words with her sketchy sweetness, and he sat there as if he had been held in a velvet vise, throbbing with the emotion, irrecoverable ever after in its freshness, of the young artist in the presence for the first time of "production" – the proofs of his book, the hanging of his picture, the rehearsal of his play. When she had finished he asked again for the same delight, and then for more music and for more; it did him such a world of good, kept him quiet and safe, smoothed out the creases of his spirit. She dropped her own experiments and gave him immortal things, and he lounged there, pacified and charmed, feeling the mean little room grow large and vague and happy possibilities come back. Abruptly, at the piano, she called out to him: "Those papers of yours – the letters you found – are not in the house?"

"No, they're not in the house."

"I was sure of it! No matter – it's all right!" she added. She herself was pacified – trouble was a false note. Later he was on the point of asking her how she knew the objects she had mentioned were not in the house; but he let it pass. The subject was a profitless riddle – a puzzle that grew grotesquely bigger, like some monstrosity seen in the darkness, as one opened one's eyes to it. He closed his eyes – he wanted another vision. Besides, she had shown him that she had extraordinary senses – her explanation would have been stranger than the fact. Moreover they had other things to talk about, in particular the question of her putting off her return to Dover till the morrow and dispensing meanwhile with the valuable protection of Sidney. This was indeed but another face of the question of her dining with him somewhere that evening (where else should she dine?) – accompanying him, for instance, just for an hour of Bohemia, in their deadly respectable lives, to a jolly little place in Soho. Mrs. Ryves declined to have her life abused, but in fact, at the proper moment, at the jolly little place, to which she did accompany him – it dealt in macaroni and Chianti – the pair put their elbows on the crumpled cloth and, face to face, with their little emptied coffee cups pushed away and the young man's cigarette lighted by her command, became increasingly confidential. They went afterwards to the theater, in cheap places, and came home in "busses" and under umbrellas.

On the way back Peter Baron turned something over in his mind as he had never turned anything before; it was the question of whether, at the end, she would let him come into her sitting room for five minutes. He felt on this point a passion of suspense and impatience, and yet for what would it be but to tell her how poor he was? This was literally the moment to say it, so supremely depleted had the hour of Bohemia left him. Even Bohemia was too expensive, and yet in the course of the day his whole temper on the subject of certain fitnesses had changed. At Jersey Villas (it was near midnight, and Mrs. Ryves, scratching a light for her glimmering taper, had said: "Oh, yes, come in for a minute if you like!"), in her precarious parlor, which was indeed, after the brilliances of the evening, a return to ugliness and truth, she let him stand while he explained that he had certainly everything in the way of fame and fortune still to gain, but that youth and love and faith and energy

– to say nothing of her supreme dearness – were all on his side. Why, if one's beginnings were rough, should one add to the hardness of the conditions by giving up the dream which, if she would only hear him out, would make just the blessed difference? Whether Mrs. Ryves heard him out or not is a circumstance as to which this chronicle happens to be silent; but after he had got possession of both her hands and breathed into her face for a moment all the intensity of his tenderness – in the relief and joy of utterance he felt it carry him like a rising flood – she checked him with better reasons, with a cold, sweet afterthought in which he felt there was something deep. Her procrastinating head-shake was prettier than ever, yet it had never meant so many fears and pains – impossibilities and memories, independences and pieties, and a sort of uncomplaining ache for the ruin of a friendship that had been happy. She had liked him – if she hadn't she wouldn't have let him think so! – but she protested that she had not, in the odious vulgar sense, "encouraged" him. Moreover she couldn't talk of such things in that place, at that hour, and she begged him not to make her regret her good nature in staying over. There were peculiarities in her position, considerations insurmountable. She got rid of him with kind and confused words, and afterwards, in the dull, humiliated night, he felt that he had been put in his place. Women in her situation, women who after having really loved and lost, usually lived on into the new dawns in which old ghosts steal away. But there was something in his whimsical neighbor that struck him as terribly invulnerable.

Chapter VII

"I've had time to look a little further into what we're prepared to do, and I find the case is one in which I should consider the advisability of going to an extreme length," said Mr. Locket. Jersey Villas the next morning had had the privilege of again receiving the editor of the Promiscuous, and he sat once more at the davenport, where the bone of contention, in the shape of a large, loose heap of papers that showed how much they had been handled, was placed well in view. "We shall see our way to offering you three hundred, but we shouldn't, I must positively assure you, see it a single step further."

Peter Baron, in his dressing gown and slippers, with his hands in his pockets, crept softly about the room, repeating, below his breath and with inflections that for his own sake he endeavored to make humorous: "Three hundred – three hundred." His state of mind was far from hilarious, for he felt poor and sore and disappointed; but he wanted to prove to himself that he was gallant – was made, in general and in particular, of undiscourageable stuff. The first thing he had been aware of on stepping into his front room was that a four-wheeled cab, with Mrs. Ryves's luggage upon it, stood at the door of No. 3. Permitting himself, behind his curtain, a pardonable peep, he saw the mistress of his thoughts come out of the house, attended by Mrs. Bundy, and take her place in the modest vehicle. After this his eyes rested for a long time on the sprigged cotton back of the landlady, who kept bobbing at the window of the cab an endlessly moralizing old head. Mrs. Ryves had really taken flight – he had made Jersey Villas impossible for her – but Mrs. Bundy, with a magnanimity unprecedented in the profession, seemed to express a belief in the purity of her motives. Baron felt that his own separation had been, for the present at least, effected; every instinct of delicacy prompted him to stand back.

Mr. Locket talked a long time, and Peter Baron listened and waited. He reflected that his willingness to listen would probably excite hopes in his visitor – hopes which he himself was ready to contemplate without a scruple. He felt no pity for Mr. Locket and had no consideration for his suspense or for his possible illusions; he only felt sick and forsaken and in want of comfort and of money. Yet it was a kind of outrage to his dignity to have the knife held to his throat, and he was irritated above all by the ground on which Mr. Locket put the question – the ground of a service rendered to historical truth. It might be – he wasn't clear; it might be – the question was deep, too deep, probably, for his wisdom; at any rate he had to control himself not to interrupt angrily such dry, interested palaver, the false voice of commerce and of cant. He stared tragically out of the window and saw the stupid rain begin to fall; the day was duller even than his own soul, and Jersey Villas looked so sordidly hideous that it was no wonder Mrs. Ryves couldn't endure them. Hideous as they were he should have to tell Mrs. Bundy in the course of the day that he was obliged to seek humbler quarters. Suddenly he interrupted Mr. Locket; he observed to him: "I take it that if I should make you this concession the hospitality of the Promiscuous would be by that very fact unrestrictedly secured to me."

Mr. Locket stared. "Hospitality – secured?" He thumbed the proposition as if it were a hard peach.

"I mean that of course you wouldn't – in courtesy, in gratitude – keep on declining my things."

"I should give them my best attention – as I've always done in the past."

Peter Baron hesitated. It was a case in which there would have seemed to be some chance for the ideally shrewd aspirant in such an advantage as he possessed; but after a moment the blood rushed into his face with the shame of the idea of pleading for his productions in the name of anything but their merit. It was as if he had stupidly uttered evil of them. Nevertheless be added the interrogation:

"Would you for instance publish my little story?"

"The one I read (and objected to some features of) the other day? Do you mean – a – with the alteration?" Mr. Locket continued.

"Oh, no, I mean utterly without it. The pages you want altered contain, as I explained to you very lucidly, I think, the very raison d'etre of the work, and it would therefore, it seems to me, be an imbecility of the first magnitude to cancel them." Peter had really renounced all hope that his critic would understand what he meant, but, under favor of circumstances, he couldn't forbear to taste the luxury, which probably never again would come within his reach, of being really plain, for one wild moment, with an editor.

Mr. Locket gave a constrained smile. "Think of the scandal, Mr. Baron."

"But isn't this other scandal just what you're going in for?"

"It will be a great public service."

"You mean it will be a big scandal, whereas my poor story would be a very small one, and that it's only out of a big one that money's to be made."

Mr. Locket got up – he too had his dignity to vindicate. "Such a sum as I offer you ought really to be an offset against all claims."

"Very good – I don't mean to make any, since you don't really care for what I write. I take note of your offer," Peter pursued, "and I engage to give you tonight (in a few words left by my own hand at your house) my absolutely definite and final reply."

Mr. Locket's movements, as he hovered near the relics of the eminent statesman, were those of some feathered parent fluttering over a threatened nest. If he had brought his huddled brood back with him this morning it was because he had felt sure enough of closing the bargain to be able to be graceful. He kept a glittering eye on the papers and remarked that he was afraid that before leaving them he must elicit some assurance that in the meanwhile Peter would not place them in any other hands. Peter, at this, gave a laugh of harsher cadence than he intended, asking, justly enough, on what privilege his visitor rested such a demand and why he himself was disqualified from offering his wares to the highest bidder. "Surely you wouldn't hawk such things about?" cried Mr. Locket; but before Baron had time to retort cynically he added: "I'll publish your little story."

"Oh, thank you!"

"I'll publish anything you'll send me," Mr. Locket continued, as he went out. Peter had before this virtually given his word that for the letters he would treat only with the Promiscuous.

The young man passed, during a portion of the rest of the day, the strangest hours of his life. Yet he thought of them afterwards not as a phase of temptation, though they had been full of the emotion that accompanies an intense vision of alternatives. The struggle was already over; it seemed to him that, poor as he was, he was not poor enough to take Mr. Locket's money. He looked at the opposed courses with the self-possession of a man who has chosen, but this self-possession was in itself the most exquisite of excitements. It was really a high revulsion and a sort of noble pity. He seemed indeed to have his finger upon the pulse of history and to be in the secret of the gods. He had them all in his hand, the tablets and the scales and the torch. He couldn't keep a character together, but he might easily pull one to pieces. That would be "creative work" of a kind – he could reconstruct the character less pleasingly, could show an unknown side of it. Mr. Locket had had a good deal to say about responsibility; and responsibility in truth sat there with him all the morning, while he revolved in his narrow cage and, watching the crude spring rain on the windows, thought of the dismalness to which, at Dover, Mrs. Ryves was going back. This influence took in fact the form, put on the physiognomy of poor Sir Dominick Ferrand; he was at present as perceptible in it, as coldly and strangely personal, as if he had been a haunting ghost and had risen beside his own old hearthstone. Our friend was accustomed to his company and indeed had spent so many hours in it of late, following him up at the museum and comparing his different portraits, engravings and lithographs, in which there seemed to be conscious, pleading eyes for the betrayer, that their queer intimacy had grown as close as an embrace. Sir Dominick was very dumb, but he was terrible in his dependence, and Peter would not have encouraged him by so much curiosity nor reassured him by so much deference had it not been for the young man's complete acceptance of the impossibility of getting out of a tight place by exposing an individual. It didn't matter that the individual was dead; it didn't matter that he was dishonest. Peter felt him sufficiently alive to suffer; he perceived the rectification of history so conscientiously desired by Mr. Locket to be somehow for himself not an imperative task. It had come over him too definitely that in a case where one's success was to hinge upon an act of extradition it would minister most to an easy conscience to let the success go. No, no – even should he be starving he couldn't make money out of Sir Dominick's disgrace. He was almost surprised at the violence of the horror with which, as he shuffled mournfully about, the idea of any such profit inspired him. What was Sir Dominick to him after all? He wished he had never come across him.

In one of his brooding pauses at the window – the window out of which never again apparently should he see Mrs. Ryves glide across the little garden with the step for which he had liked her from the first – he became aware that the rain was about to intermit and the sun to make some grudging amends. This was a sign that he might go out; he had a vague perception that there were things to be done. He had work to look for, and a cheaper lodging, and a new idea (every idea he had ever cherished had left him), in addition to which the promised little word was to be dropped at Mr. Locket's door. He looked at his watch and was surprised at the hour, for he had nothing but a heartache to show for so much time. He would have to dress quickly, but as he passed to his bedroom his eye was caught by the little pyramid of letters which Mr. Locket had constructed on his davenport. They startled him and, staring at them, he stopped for an instant, half-amused, half-annoyed at their being still in existence. He had so completely destroyed them in spirit that he had taken the act for granted, and he was now reminded of the orderly stages of which an intention must consist to be sincere. Baron went at the papers with all his sincerity, and at his empty grate (where there lately had been no fire and he had only to remove a horrible ornament of tissue-paper dear to Mrs. Bundy) he burned the collection with infinite method. It made him feel happier to watch the worst pages turn to illegible ashes – if happiness be the right word to apply to his sense, in the process, of something so crisp and crackling that it suggested the death-rustle of bank-notes.

When ten minutes later he came back into his sitting room, he seemed to himself oddly, unexpectedly in the presence of a bigger view. It was as if some interfering mass had been so displaced that he could see more sky and more country. Yet the opposite houses were naturally still there, and if the grimy little place looked lighter it was doubtless only because the rain had indeed stopped and the sun was pouring in. Peter went to the window to open it to the altered air, and in doing so beheld at the garden gate the humble "growler" in which a few hours before he had seen Mrs. Ryves take her departure. It was unmistakable – he remembered the knock-kneed white horse; but this made the fact that his friend's luggage no longer surmounted it only the more mystifying. Perhaps the cabman had already removed the luggage – he was now on his box smoking the short pipe that derived relish from inaction paid for. As Peter turned into the room again his ears caught a knock at his own door, a knock explained, as soon as he had responded, by the hard breathing of Mrs. Bundy.

"Please, sir, it's to say she've come back."

"What has she come back for?" Baron's question sounded ungracious, but his heartache had given another throb, and he felt a dread of another wound. It was like a practical joke.

"I think it's for you, sir," said Mrs. Bundy. "She'll see you for a moment, if you'll be so good, in the old place."

Peter followed his hostess downstairs, and Mrs. Bundy ushered him, with her company flourish, into the apartment she had fondly designated.

"I went away this morning, and I've only returned for an instant," said Mrs. Ryves, as soon as Mrs. Bundy had closed the door. He saw that she was different now; something had happened that had made her indulgent.

"Have you been all the way to Dover and back?"

"No, but I've been to Victoria. I've left my luggage there – I've been driving about."

"I hope you've enjoyed it."

"Very much. I've been to see Mr. Morrish."

"Mr. Morrish?"

"The musical publisher. I showed him our song. I played it for him, and he's delighted with it. He declares it's just the thing. He has given me fifty pounds. I think he believes in us," Mrs. Ryves went on, while Baron stared at the wonder – too sweet to be safe, it seemed to him as yet – of her standing there again before him and speaking of what they had in common. "Fifty pounds! fifty pounds!" she exclaimed, fluttering at him her happy check. She had come back, the first thing, to tell him, and of course his share of the money would be the half. She was rosy, jubilant, natural, she chattered like a happy woman. She said they must do more, ever so much more. Mr. Morrish had practically promised he would take anything that was as good as that. She had kept her cab because she was going to Dover; she couldn't leave the others alone. It was a vehicle infirm and inert, but Baron, after a little, appreciated its pace, for she had consented to his getting in with her and driving, this time in earnest, to Victoria. She had only come to tell him the good news – she repeated this assurance more than once. They talked of it so profoundly that it drove everything else for the time out of his head – his duty to Mr. Locket, the remarkable sacrifice he had just achieved, and even the odd coincidence, matching with the oddity of all the others, of her having reverted to the house again, as if with one of her famous divinations, at the very moment the trumpery papers, the origin really of their intimacy, had ceased to exist. But she, on her side, also had evidently forgotten the trumpery papers: she never mentioned them again, and Peter Baron never boasted of what he had done with them. He was silent for a while, from curiosity to see if her fine nerves had really given her a hint; and then later, when it came to be a question of his permanent attitude, he was silent, prodigiously, religiously, tremulously silent, in consequence of an extraordinary conversation that he had with her.

This conversation took place at Dover, when he went down to give her the money for which, at Mr. Morrish's bank, he had exchanged the check she had left with him. That check, or rather certain things it represented, had made somehow all the difference in their relations. The difference was huge, and Baron could think of nothing but this confirmed vision of their being able to work fruitfully together that would account for so rapid a change. She didn't talk of impossibilities now – she didn't seem to want to stop him off; only when, the day following his arrival at Dover with the fifty pounds (he had after all to agree to share them with her – he couldn't expect her to take a present of money from him), he returned to the question over which they had had their little scene the night they dined together – on this occasion (he had brought a portmanteau and he was staying) she mentioned that there was something very particular she had it on her conscience to tell him before letting him commit himself. There dawned in her face as she approached the subject a light of warning that frightened him; it was charged with something so strange that for an instant he held his breath. This flash of ugly possibilities passed however, and it was with the gesture of taking still tenderer possession of her, checked indeed by the grave, important way she held up a finger, that he answered: "Tell me everything – tell me!"

"You must know what I am – who I am; you must know especially what I'm not! There's a name for it, a hideous, cruel name. It's not my fault! Others have known, I've had to speak of it – it has made a great difference in my life. Surely you must have guessed!" she went on, with the thinnest quaver of irony, letting him now take her hand, which felt as cold as her hard duty. "Don't you see I've no belongings, no relations, no friends, nothing at all, in all the world, of my own? I was only a poor girl."

"A poor girl?" Baron was mystified, touched, distressed, piecing dimly together what she meant, but feeling, in a great surge of pity, that it was only something more to love her for.

"My mother – my poor mother," said Mrs. Ryves.

She paused with this, and through gathering tears her eyes met his as if to plead with him to understand. He understood, and drew her closer, but she kept herself free still, to continue: "She was a poor girl – she was only a governess; she was alone, she thought he loved her. He did – I think it was the only happiness she ever knew. But she died of it."

"Oh, I'm so glad you tell me – it's so grand of you!" Baron murmured. "Then – your father?" He hesitated, as if with his hands on old wounds.

"He had his own troubles, but he was kind to her. It was all misery and folly – he was married. He wasn't happy – there were good reasons, I believe, for that. I know it from letters, I know it from a person who's dead. Everyone is dead now – it's too far off. That's the only good thing. He was very kind to me; I remember him, though I didn't know then, as a little girl, who he was. He put me with some very good people – he did what he could for me. I think, later, his wife knew – a lady who came to see me once after his death. I was a very little girl, but I remember many things. What he could he did – something that helped me afterwards, something that helps me now. I think of him with a strange pity – I *see* him!" said Mrs. Ryves, with the faint past in her eyes. "You mustn't say anything against him," she added, gently and gravely.

"Never – never; for he has only made it more of a rapture to care for you."

"You must wait, you must think; we must wait together," she went on. "You can't tell, and you must give me time. Now that you know, it's all right; but you had to know. Doesn't it make us better friends?" asked Mrs. Ryves, with a tired smile which had the effect of putting the whole story further and further away. The next moment, however, she added quickly, as if with the sense that it couldn't be far enough: "You don't know, you can't judge, you must let it settle. Think of it, think of it; oh you will, and leave it so. I must have time myself, oh I must! Yes, you must believe me."

She turned away from him, and he remained looking at her a moment. "Ah, how I shall work for you!" he exclaimed.

"You must work for yourself; I'll help you." Her eyes had met his eyes again, and she added, hesitating, thinking: "You had better know, perhaps, who he was."

Baron shook his head, smiling confidently. "I don't care a straw."

"I do – a little. He was a great man."

"There must indeed have been some good in him."

"He was a high celebrity. You've often heard of him."

Baron wondered an instant. "I've no doubt you're a princess!" he said with a laugh. She made him nervous.

"I'm not ashamed of him. He was Sir Dominick Ferrand."

Baron saw in her face, in a few seconds, that she had seen something in his. He knew that he stared, then turned pale; it had the effect of a powerful shock. He was cold for an instant, as he had just found her, with the sense of danger, the confused horror of having dealt a blow. But the blood rushed back to its courses with his still quicker consciousness of safety, and he could make out, as he recovered his balance, that his emotion struck her simply as a violent surprise. He gave a muffled murmur: "Ah, it's you, my beloved!" which lost itself as he drew her close and held her long, in the intensity of his embrace and the wonder of his escape. It took more than a minute for him to say over to himself often enough, with his hidden face: "Ah, she must never, never know!"

She never knew; she only learned, when she asked him casually, that he had in fact destroyed the old documents she had had such a comic caprice about. The sensibility, the curiosity they had had the queer privilege of exciting in her had lapsed with the event as irresponsibly as they had arisen, and she appeared to have forgotten, or rather to attribute now to other causes, the agitation and several of the odd incidents that accompanied them. They naturally gave Peter Baron rather more to think about, much food, indeed, for clandestine meditation, some of which, in spite of the pains he took not to be caught, was noted by his friend and interpreted, to his knowledge, as depression produced by the long probation she succeeded in imposing on him. He was more patient than she could guess, with all her guessing, for if he was put to the proof she herself was not left undissected. It came back to him again and again that if the documents he had burned proved anything they proved that Sir Dominick Ferrand's human errors were not all of one order. The woman he loved was the daughter of her father, he couldn't get over that. What was more to the point was that as he came to know her better and better – for they did work together under Mr. Morrish's protection – his affection was a quantity still less to be neglected. He sometimes wondered, in the light of her general straightness (their marriage had brought out even more than he believed there was of it) whether the relics in the davenport were genuine. That piece of furniture is still almost as useful to him as Mr. Morrish's patronage. There is a tremendous run, as this gentlemen calls it, on several of their songs. Baron nevertheless still tries his hand also at prose, and his offerings are now not always declined by the magazines. But he has never approached the Promiscuous again. This periodical published in due course a highly eulogistic study of the remarkable career of Sir Dominick Ferrand.

Nona Vincent

Chapter I

"I wondered whether you wouldn't read it to me," said Mrs. Alsager, as they lingered a little near the fire before he took leave. She looked down at the fire sideways, drawing her dress away from it and making her proposal with a shy sincerity that added to her charm. Her charm was always great for Allan Wayworth, and the whole air of her house, which was simply a sort of distillation of herself, so soothing, so beguiling that he always made several false starts before departure. He had spent some such good hours there, had forgotten, in her warm, golden drawing room, so much of the loneliness and so many of the worries of his life, that it had come to be the immediate answer to his longings, the cure for his aches, the harbor of refuge from his storms. His tribulations were not unprecedented, and some of his advantages, if of a usual kind, were marked in degree, inasmuch as he was very clever for one so young, and very independent for one so poor. He was eight-and-twenty, but he had lived a good deal and was full of ambitions and curiosities and disappointments. The opportunity to talk of some of these in Grosvenor Place corrected perceptibly the immense inconvenience of London. This inconvenience took for him principally the line of insensibility to Allan Wayworth's literary form. He had a literary form, or he thought he had, and her intelligent recognition of the circumstance was the sweetest consolation Mrs. Alsager could have administered. She was even more literary and more artistic than he, inasmuch as he could often work off his overflow (this was his occupation, his profession), while the generous woman, abounding in happy thoughts, but unedited and unpublished, stood there in the rising tide like the nymph of a fountain in the plash of the marble basin.

The year before, in a big newspapery house, he had found himself next her at dinner, and they had converted the intensely material hour into a feast of reason. There was no motive for her asking him to come to see her but that she liked him, which it was the more agreeable to him to perceive as he perceived at the same time that she was exquisite. She was enviably free to act upon her likings, and it made Wayworth feel less unsuccessful to infer that for the moment he happened to be one of them. He kept the revelation to himself, and indeed there was nothing to turn his head in the kindness of a kind woman. Mrs. Alsager occupied so completely the ground of possession that she would have been condemned to inaction had it not been for the principle of giving. Her husband, who was twenty years her senior, a massive personality in the City and a heavy one at home (wherever he stood, or even sat, he was monumental), owned half a big newspaper and the whole of a great many other things. He admired his wife, though she bore no children, and liked her to have other tastes than his, as that seemed to give a greater acreage to their life. His own appetites went so far he could scarcely see the boundary, and his theory was to trust her to push the limits of hers, so that between them the pair should astound by their consumption. His ideas were prodigiously vulgar, but some of them had the good fortune to be carried out by a person of perfect delicacy. Her delicacy made her play strange tricks with them, but he never found this out. She attenuated him without his knowing it, for what he mainly thought was that he had aggrandized *her.* Without her he really would have been bigger still, and society, breathing more freely, was practically under an obligation to her which, to do it justice, it acknowledged by an attitude of mystified respect. She felt a tremulous need to throw her liberty and her leisure into the things of the soul – the most beautiful things she knew. She found them, when she gave time to seeking, in a hundred places, and particularly in a dim and sacred region – the region of active pity – over her entrance into which she dropped curtains so thick that it would have been an impertinence to lift them. But she cultivated other beneficent passions, and if she cherished the dream of something fine the moments at which it most seemed to her to come true were when she saw beauty plucked flowerlike in the garden of art. She loved the perfect work – she had the artistic chord. This chord could vibrate only to the touch of another, so that appreciation, in her spirit, had the added intensity of regret. She could understand the joy of creation, and she thought it scarcely enough to be told that she herself created happiness. She would have liked, at any rate, to choose her way; but it was just here that her liberty failed her. She had not the voice – she had only the vision. The only envy she was capable of was directed to those who, as she said, could do something.

As everything in her, however, turned to gentleness, she was admirably hospitable to such people as a class. She believed Allan Wayworth could do something, and she liked to hear him talk of the ways in which he meant to show it. He talked of them almost to no one else – she spoiled him for other listeners. With her fair bloom and her quiet grace she was indeed an ideal public, and if she had ever confided to him that she would have liked to scribble (she had in fact not mentioned it to a creature), he would have been in a perfect position for asking her why a woman whose face had so much expression should not have felt that she achieved. How in the world could she express better? There was less than that in Shakespeare and Beethoven. She had never been more generous than when, in compliance with her invitation, which I have recorded, he brought his play to read to her. He had spoken of it to her before, and one dark November afternoon, when her red fireside was more than ever an escape from the place and the season, he had broken out as he came in – "I've done it, I've done it!" She made him tell her all about it – she took an interest really minute and asked questions delightfully apt. She had spoken from the first as if he were on the point of being acted, making him jump, with her participation, all sorts of dreary intervals. She liked the theater as she liked all the arts of expression, and he had known her to go all the way to Paris for a particular performance. Once he had gone with her – the time she took that stupid Mrs. Mostyn. She had been struck, when he sketched it, with the subject of his drama, and had spoken words that helped him to believe in it. As soon as he had rung down his curtain on the last act he rushed off to see her, but after that he kept the thing for repeated last touches. Finally, on Christmas day, by arrangement, she sat there and listened to it. It was in three acts and in prose, but rather of the romantic order, though dealing with contemporary English life, and he fondly believed that it showed the hand if not of the master, at least of the prize pupil.

Allan Wayworth had returned to England, at two-and-twenty, after a miscellaneous continental education; his father, the correspondent, for years, in several foreign countries successively, of a conspicuous London journal, had died just after this, leaving his mother and her two other children, portionless girls, to subsist on a very small income in a very dull German town. The young man's beginnings in London were difficult, and he had aggravated them by his dislike of journalism. His father's connection with it would have helped him, but he was (insanely, most of his friends judged – the great exception was always Mrs. Alsager) *intraitable* on the question of form. Form – in his sense – was not demanded by English newspapers, and he couldn't give it to them in *their* sense. The demand for it was not great anywhere, and Wayworth spent costly weeks in polishing little compositions for magazines that didn't pay for style. The only person who paid for it was really Mrs. Alsager: she had an infallible instinct for the perfect. She paid in her own way, and if Allan Wayworth had been a wage-earning person it would have made him feel that if he didn't receive his legal dues his palm was at least occasionally conscious of a gratuity. He had his limitations, his perversities, but the finest parts of him were the most alive, and he was restless and sincere. It is however the impression he produced on Mrs. Alsager that most concerns us: she thought him not only remarkably good-looking but altogether original. There were some usual bad things he would never do – too many prohibitive puddles for him in the short cut to success.

For himself, he had never been so happy as since he had seen his way, as he fondly believed, to some sort of mastery of the scenic idea, which struck him as a very different matter now that he looked at it from within. He had had his early days of contempt for it, when it seemed to him a jewel, dim at the best, hidden in a dunghill, a taper burning low in an air thick with vulgarity. It was hedged about with sordid approaches, it was not worth sacrifice and suffering. The man of letters, in dealing with it, would have to put off all literature, which was like asking the bearer of a noble name to forego his immemorial heritage. Aspects change, however, with the point of view: Wayworth had waked up one morning in a different bed altogether. It is needless here to trace this accident to its source; it would have been much more interesting to a spectator of the young man's life to follow some of the consequences. He had been made (as he felt) the subject of a special revelation, and he wore his hat like a man in love. An angel had taken him by the hand and guided him to the shabby door which opens, it appeared, into an interior both splendid and austere. The scenic idea was magnificent when once you had embraced it – the dramatic form had a purity which made some others look ingloriously rough. It had the high dignity of the exact sciences, it was mathematical and architectural. It was full of the refreshment of calculation and construction, the incorruptibility of line and law. It was bare, but it was erect, it was poor, but it was noble; it reminded him of some sovereign famed for justice who should have lived in a palace despoiled. There was a fearful amount of concession in it, but what you kept had a rare intensity. You were perpetually throwing over the cargo to save the ship, but what a motion you gave her when you made her ride the waves – a motion as rhythmic as the dance of a goddess! Wayworth took long London walks and thought of these things – London poured into his ears the mighty hum of its suggestion. His imagination glowed and melted down material, his intentions multiplied and made the air a golden haze. He saw not only the thing he should do, but the next and the next and the next; the future opened before him and he seemed to walk on marble slabs. The more he tried the dramatic form the more he loved it, the more he looked at it the more he perceived in it. What he perceived in it indeed he now perceived everywhere; if he stopped, in the London dusk, before some flaring shop window, the place immediately constituted itself behind footlights, became a framed stage for his figures. He hammered at these figures in his lonely lodging, he shaped them and he shaped their tabernacle; he was like a goldsmith chiseling a casket, bent over with the passion for perfection. When he was neither roaming the streets with his vision nor worrying his problem at his table, he was exchanging ideas on the general question with Mrs. Alsager, to whom he promised details that would amuse her in later and still happier hours. Her eyes were full of tears when he read her the last words of the finished work, and she murmured, divinely -

"And now – to get it done, to get it done!"

"Yes, indeed – to get it done!" Wayworth stared at the fire, slowly rolling up his type-copy. "But that's a totally different part of the business, and altogether secondary."

"But of course you want to be acted?"

"Of course I do – but it's a sudden descent. I want to intensely, but I'm sorry I want to."

"It's there indeed that the difficulties begin," said Mrs. Alsager, a little off her guard.

"How can you say that? It's there that they end!"

"Ah, wait to see where they end!"

"I mean they'll now be of a totally different order," Wayworth explained. "It seems to me there can be nothing in the world more difficult than to write a play that will stand an all-round test, and that in comparison with them the complications that spring up at this point are of an altogether smaller kind."

"Yes, they're not inspiring," said Mrs. Alsager; "they're discouraging, because they're vulgar. The other problem, the working out of the thing itself, is pure art."

"How well you understand everything!" The young man had got up, nervously, and was leaning against the chimneypiece with his back to the fire and his arms folded. The roll of his copy, in his fist, was squeezed into the hollow of one of them. He looked down at Mrs. Alsager, smiling gratefully, and she answered him with a smile from eyes still charmed and suffused. "Yes, the vulgarity will begin now," he presently added.

"You'll suffer dreadfully."

"I shall suffer in a good cause."

"Yes, giving *that* to the world! You must leave it with me, I must read it over and over," Mrs. Alsager pleaded, rising to come nearer and draw the copy, in its cover of greenish-grey paper, which had a generic identity now to him, out of his grasp. "Who in the world will do it? – who in the world *can?*" she went on, close to him, turning over the leaves. Before he could answer she had stopped at one of the pages; she turned the book round to him, pointing out a speech. "That's the most beautiful place – those lines are a perfection." He glanced at the spot she indicated, and she begged him to read them again – he had read them admirably before. He knew them by heart, and, closing the book while she held the other end of it, he murmured them over to her – they had indeed a cadence that pleased him – watching, with a facetious complacency which he hoped was pardonable, the applause in her face. "Ah, who can utter such lines as *that?*" Mrs. Alsager broke out; "whom can you find to do *her?*"

"We'll find people to do them all!"

"But not people who are worthy."

"They'll be worthy enough if they're willing enough. I'll work with them – I'll grind it into them." He spoke as if he had produced twenty plays.

"Oh, it will be interesting!" she echoed.

"But I shall have to find my theater first. I shall have to get a manager to believe in me."

"Yes – they're so stupid!"

"But fancy the patience I shall want, and how I shall have to watch and wait," said Allan Wayworth. "Do you see me hawking it about London?"

"Indeed I don't – it would be sickening."

"It's what I shall have to do. I shall be old before it's produced."

"I shall be old very soon if it isn't!" Mrs. Alsager cried. "I know one or two of them," she mused.

"Do you mean you would speak to them?"

"The thing is to get them to read it. I could do that."

"That's the utmost I ask. But it's even for that I shall have to wait."

She looked at him with kind sisterly eyes. "You shan't wait."

"Ah, you dear lady!" Wayworth murmured.

"That is *you* may, but *I* won't! Will you leave me your copy?" she went on, turning the pages again.

"Certainly; I have another." Standing near him she read to herself a passage here and there; then, in her sweet voice, she read some of them out. "Oh, if *you* were only an actress!" the young man exclaimed.

"That's the last thing I am. There's no comedy in *me!*"

She had never appeared to Wayworth so much his good genius. "Is there any tragedy?" he asked, with the levity of complete confidence.

She turned away from him, at this, with a strange and charming laugh and a "Perhaps that will be for you to determine!" But before he could disclaim such a responsibility she had faced him again and was talking about Nona Vincent as if she had been the most interesting of their friends and her situation at that moment an irresistible appeal to their sympathy. Nona Vincent was the heroine of the play, and Mrs. Alsager had taken a tremendous fancy to her. "I can't *tell* you how I like that woman!" she exclaimed in a pensive rapture of credulity which could only be balm to the artistic spirit.

"I'm awfully glad she lives a bit. What I feel about her is that she's a good deal like *you,*" Wayworth observed.

Mrs. Alsager stared an instant and turned faintly red. This was evidently a view that failed to strike her; she didn't, however, treat it as a joke. "I'm not impressed with the resemblance. I don't see myself doing what she does."

"It isn't so much what she *does,*" the young man argued, drawing out his moustache.

"But what she does is the whole point. She simply tells her love – I should never do that."

"If you repudiate such a proceeding with such energy, why do you like her for it?"

"It isn't what I like her for."

"What else, then? That's intensely characteristic."

Mrs. Alsager reflected, looking down at the fire; she had the air of having half-a-dozen reasons to choose from. But the one she produced was unexpectedly simple; it might even have been prompted by despair at not finding others. "I like her because *you* made her!" she exclaimed with a laugh, moving again away from her companion.

Wayworth laughed still louder. "You made her a little yourself. I've thought of her as looking like you."

"She ought to look much better," said Mrs. Alsager. "No, certainly, I shouldn't do what *she* does."

"Not even in the same circumstances?"

"I should never find myself in such circumstances. They're exactly your play, and have nothing in common with such a life as mine. However," Mrs. Alsager went on, "her behavior was natural for *her,* and not only natural, but, it seems to me, thoroughly beautiful and noble. I can't sufficiently admire the talent and tact with which you make one accept it, and I tell you frankly that it's evident to me there must be a brilliant future before a young man who, at the start, has been capable of such a stroke as that. Thank heaven I can admire Nona Vincent as intensely as I feel that I don't resemble her!"

"Don't exaggerate that," said Allan Wayworth.

"My admiration?"

"Your dissimilarity. She has your face, your air, your voice, your motion; she has many elements of your being."

"Then she'll damn your play!" Mrs. Alsager replied. They joked a little over this, though it was not in the tone of pleasantry that Wayworth's hostess soon remarked: "You've got your remedy, however: have her done by the right woman."

"Oh, have her 'done' – have her 'done'!" the young man gently wailed.

"I see what you mean, my poor friend. What a pity, when it's such a magnificent part – such a chance for a clever serious girl! Nona Vincent is practically your play – it will be open to her to carry it far or to drop it at the first corner."

"It's a charming prospect," said Allan Wayworth, with sudden skepticism. They looked at each other with eyes that, for a lurid moment, saw the worst of the worst; but before they parted they had exchanged vows and confidences that were dedicated wholly to the ideal. It is not to be supposed, however, that the knowledge that Mrs. Alsager would help him made Wayworth less eager to help himself. He did what he could and felt that she, on her side, was doing no less; but at the end of a year he was obliged to recognize that their united effort had mainly produced the fine flower of discouragement. At the end of a year the luster had, to his own eyes, quite faded from his unappreciated masterpiece, and he found himself writing for a biographical dictionary little lives of celebrities he had never heard of. To be printed, anywhere and anyhow, was a form of glory for a man so unable to be acted, and to be paid, even at encyclopedic rates, had the consequence of making one resigned and verbose. He couldn't smuggle style into a dictionary, but he could at least reflect that he had done his best to learn from the drama that it is a gross impertinence almost anywhere. He had knocked at the door of every theater in London, and, at a ruinous expense, had multiplied type-copies of Nona Vincent to replace the neat transcripts that had descended into the managerial abyss. His play was not even declined – no such flattering intimation was given him that it had been read. What the managers would do for Mrs. Alsager concerned him little today; the thing that was relevant was that they would do nothing for *him.* That charming woman felt humbled to the earth, so little response had she had from the powers on which she counted. The two never talked about the play now, but he tried to show her a still finer friendship, that she might not think he felt she had failed him. He still walked about London with his dreams, but as months succeeded months and he left the year behind him they were dreams not so much of success as of revenge. Success seemed a colorless name for the reward of his patience; something fiercely florid, something sanguinolent was more to the point. His best consolation however was still in the scenic idea; it was not till now that he discovered how incurably he was in love with it. By the time a vain second year had chafed itself away he cherished his fruitless faculty the more for the obloquy it seemed to suffer. He lived, in his best hours, in a world of subjects and situations; he wrote another play and made it as different from its predecessor as such a very good thing could be. It might be a very good thing, but when he had committed it to the theatrical limbo indiscriminating fate took no account of the difference. He was at last able to leave England for three or four months; he went to Germany to pay a visit long deferred to his mother and sisters.

Shortly before the time he had fixed for his return he received from Mrs. Alsager a telegram consisting of the words: "Loder wishes see you – putting Nona instant rehearsal." He spent the few hours before his departure in kissing his mother and sisters, who knew enough about Mrs. Alsager to judge it lucky this respectable married lady was not there – a relief, however, accompanied with speculative glances at London and the morrow. Loder, as our young man was aware, meant the new "Renaissance," but though he reached home in the evening it was not to this convenient modern theater that Wayworth first proceeded. He spent a late hour with Mrs. Alsager, an hour that throbbed with calculation. She told him that Mr. Loder was charming, he had simply taken up the play in its turn; he had hopes of it, moreover, that on the part of a professional pessimist might almost be qualified as ecstatic. It had been cast, with a margin for objections, and Violet Grey was to do the heroine. She had been capable, while he was away, of a good piece of work at that foggy old playhouse the "Legitimate;" the piece was a clumsy rechauffe, but she at least had been fresh. Wayworth remembered Violet Grey – hadn't he, for two years, on a fond policy of "looking out," kept dipping into the London theaters to pick up prospective interpreters? He had not picked up many as yet, and this young lady at all events had never wriggled in his net. She was pretty and she was odd, but he had never prefigured her as Nona Vincent, nor indeed found himself attracted by what he already felt sufficiently launched in the profession to speak of as her artistic personality. Mrs. Alsager was different – she declared that she had been struck not a little by some of her tones. The girl was interesting in the thing at the "Legitimate," and

Mr. Loder, who had his eye on her, described her as ambitious and intelligent. She wanted awfully to get on – and some of those ladies were so lazy! Wayworth was skeptical – he had seen Miss Violet Grey, who was terribly itinerant, in a dozen theaters but only in one aspect. Nona Vincent had a dozen aspects, but only one theater; yet with what a feverish curiosity the young man promised himself to watch the actress on the morrow! Talking the matter over with Mrs. Alsager now seemed the very stuff that rehearsal was made of. The near prospect of being acted laid a finger even on the lip of inquiry; he wanted to go on tiptoe till the first night, to make no condition but that they should speak his lines, and he felt that he wouldn't so much as raise an eyebrow at the scene-painter if he should give him an old oak chamber.

He became conscious, the next day, that his danger would be other than this, and yet he couldn't have expressed to himself what it would be. Danger was there, doubtless – danger was everywhere, in the world of art, and still more in the world of commerce; but what he really seemed to catch, for the hour, was the beating of the wings of victory. Nothing could undermine that, since it was victory simply to be acted. It would be victory even to be acted badly; a reflection that didn't prevent him, however, from banishing, in his politic optimism, the word "bad" from his vocabulary. It had no application, in the compromise of practice; it didn't apply even to his play, which he was conscious he had already outlived and as to which he foresaw that, in the coming weeks, frequent alarm would alternate, in his spirit, with frequent esteem. When he went down to the dusky daylit theater (it arched over him like the temple of fame) Mr. Loder, who was as charming as Mrs. Alsager had announced, struck him as the genius of hospitality. The manager began to explain why, for so long, he had given no sign; but that was the last thing that interested Wayworth now, and he could never remember afterwards what reasons Mr. Loder had enumerated. He liked, in the whole business of discussion and preparation, even the things he had thought he should probably dislike, and he reveled in those he had thought he should like. He watched Miss Violet Grey that evening with eyes that sought to penetrate her possibilities. She certainly had a few; they were qualities of voice and face, qualities perhaps even of intelligence; he sat there at any rate with a fostering, coaxing attention, repeating over to himself as convincingly as he could that she was not common – a circumstance all the more creditable as the part she was playing seemed to him desperately so. He perceived that this was why it pleased the audience; he divined that it was the part they enjoyed rather than the actress. He had a private panic, wondering how, if they liked *that* form, they could possibly like his. His form had now become quite an ultimate idea to him. By the time the evening was over some of Miss Violet Grey's features, several of the turns of her head, a certain vibration of her voice, had taken their place in the same category. She *was* interesting, she was distinguished; at any rate he had accepted her: it came to the same thing. But he left the theater that night without speaking to her – moved (a little even to his own mystification) by an odd procrastinating impulse. On the morrow he was to read his three acts to the company, and then he should have a good deal to say; what he felt for the moment was a vague indisposition to commit himself. Moreover he found a slight confusion of annoyance in the fact that though he had been trying all the evening to look at Nona Vincent in Violet Grey's person, what subsisted in his vision was simply Violet Grey in Nona's. He didn't wish to see the actress so directly, or even so simply as that; and it had been very fatiguing, the effort to focus Nona both through the performer and through the "Legitimate." Before he went to bed that night he posted three words to Mrs. Alsager – "She's not a bit like it, but I dare say I can make her do."

He was pleased with the way the actress listened, the next day, at the reading; he was pleased indeed with many things, at the reading, and most of all with the reading itself. The whole affair loomed large to him and he magnified it and mapped it out. He enjoyed his occupation of the big, dim, hollow theater, full of the echoes of "effect" and of a queer smell of gas and success – it all seemed such a passive canvas for his picture. For the first time in his life he was in command of resources; he was acquainted with the phrase, but had never thought he should know the feeling. He was surprised at what Loder appeared ready to do, though he reminded himself that he must never show it. He foresaw that there would be two distinct concomitants to the artistic effort of producing a play, one consisting of a great deal of anguish and the other of a great deal of amusement. He looked back upon the reading, afterwards, as the best hour in the business, because it was then that the piece had most struck him as represented. What came later was the doing of others; but this, with its imperfections and failures, was all his own. The drama lived, at any rate, for that hour, with an intensity that it was promptly to lose in the poverty and patchiness of rehearsal; he could see its life reflected, in a way that was sweet to him, in the stillness of the little semi-circle of attentive and inscrutable, of waterproofed and muddy-booted, actors. Miss Violet Grey was the auditor he had most to say to, and he tried on the spot, across the shabby stage, to let her have the soul of her part. Her attitude was graceful, but though she appeared to listen with all her faculties her face remained perfectly blank; a fact, however, not discouraging to Wayworth, who liked her better for not being premature. Her companions gave discernible signs of recognizing the passages of comedy; yet Wayworth forgave her even then for being inexpressive. She evidently wished before everything else to be simply sure of what it was all about.

He was more surprised even than at the revelation of the scale on which Mr. Loder was ready to proceed by the discovery that some of the actors didn't like their parts, and his heart sank as he asked himself what he could possibly do with them if they were going to be so stupid. This was the first of his disappointments; somehow he had expected every individual to become instantly and gratefully conscious of a rare opportunity, and from the moment such a calculation failed he was at sea, or mindful at any rate that more disappointments would come. It was impossible to make out what the manager liked or disliked; no judgment, no comment escaped him; his acceptance of the play and his views about the way it should be mounted had apparently converted him into a veiled and shrouded figure. Wayworth was able to grasp the idea that they would all move now in a higher and sharper air than that of compliment and confidence. When he talked with Violet Grey after the reading he gathered that she was really rather crude: what better proof of it could there be than her failure to break out instantly with an expression of delight about her great chance? This reserve, however, had evidently nothing to do with high pretensions; she had no wish to make him feel that a person of her eminence was superior to easy raptures. He guessed, after a little, that she was puzzled and even somewhat frightened – to a certain extent she had not understood. Nothing could appeal to him more than the opportunity to clear up her difficulties, in the course of the examination of which he quickly discovered that, so far as she *had* understood, she had understood wrong. If she was crude it was only a reason the more for talking to her; he kept saying to her "Ask me – ask me: ask me everything you can think of."

She asked him, she was perpetually asking him, and at the first rehearsals, which were without form and void to a degree that made them strike him much more as the death of an experiment than as the dawn of a success, they threshed things out immensely in a corner of the stage, with the effect of his coming to feel that at any rate she was in earnest. He felt more and more that his heroine was the keystone of his arch, for which indeed the actress was very ready to take her. But when he reminded this young lady of the way the whole thing practically depended on her she was alarmed and even slightly scandalized: she spoke more than once as if that could scarcely be the right way to construct a play – make it stand or fall by one poor nervous girl. She was almost morbidly conscientious, and in theory he liked her for this, though he lost patience three or four times with the things she couldn't do and the things she could. At such times the tears came to her eyes; but they were produced by her own stupidity, she hastened to assure him, not by the way he spoke, which was awfully kind under the circumstances. Her sincerity made her beautiful, and he wished to heaven (and made a point of telling her so) that she could sprinkle a little of it over Nona. Once, however, she was so touched and troubled that the sight of it brought the tears for an instant to his own eyes; and it so happened that, turning at this moment, he found himself face to face with Mr. Loder. The manager stared, glanced at the actress, who turned in the other direction, and then smiling at Wayworth, exclaimed, with the humor of a man who heard the gallery laugh every night:

"I say – I say!"

"What's the matter?" Wayworth asked.

"I'm glad to see Miss Grey is taking such pains with you."

"Oh, yes – she'll turn me out!" said the young man, gaily. He was quite aware that it was apparent he was not superficial about Nona, and abundantly determined, into the bargain, that the rehearsal of the piece should not sacrifice a shade of thoroughness to any extrinsic consideration.

Mrs. Alsager, whom, late in the afternoon, he used often to go and ask for a cup of tea, thanking her in advance for the rest she gave him and telling her how he found that rehearsal (as *they* were doing it – it was a caution!) took it out of one – Mrs. Alsager, more and more his good genius and, as he repeatedly assured her, his ministering angel, confirmed him in this superior policy and urged him on to every form of artistic devotion. She had, naturally, never been more interested than now in his work; she wanted to hear everything about everything. She treated him as heroically fatigued, plied him with luxurious restoratives, made him stretch himself on cushions and rose-leaves. They gossiped more than ever, by her fire, about the artistic life; he confided to her, for instance, all his hopes and fears, all his experiments and anxieties, on the subject of the representative of Nona. She was immensely interested in this young lady and showed it by taking a box again and again (she had seen her half-a-dozen times already), to study her capacity through the veil of her present part. Like Allan Wayworth she found her encouraging only by fits, for she had fine flashes of badness. She was intelligent, but she cried aloud for training, and the training was so absent that the intelligence had only a fraction of its effect. She was like a knife without an edge – good steel that had never been sharpened; she hacked away at her hard dramatic loaf, she couldn't cut it smooth.

Chapter II

"Certainly my leading lady won't make Nona much like *you!*" Wayworth one day gloomily remarked to Mrs. Alsager. There were days when the prospect seemed to him awful.

"So much the better. There's no necessity for that."

"I wish you'd train her a little – you could so easily," the young man went on; in response to which Mrs. Alsager requested him not to make such cruel fun of her. But she was curious about the girl, wanted to hear of her character, her private situation, how she lived and where, seemed indeed desirous to befriend her. Wayworth might not have known much about the private situation of Miss Violet Grey, but, as it happened, he was able, by the time his play had been three weeks in rehearsal, to supply information on such points. She was a charming, exemplary person, educated, cultivated, with highly modern tastes, an excellent musician. She had lost her parents and was very much alone in the world, her only two relations being a sister, who was married to a civil servant (in a highly responsible post) in India, and a dear little old-fashioned aunt (really a great-aunt) with whom she lived at Notting Hill, who wrote children's books and who, it appeared, had once written a Christmas pantomime. It was quite an artistic home – not on the scale of Mrs. Alsager's (to compare the smallest things with the greatest!) but intensely refined and honorable. Wayworth went so far as to hint that it would be rather nice and human on Mrs. Alsager's part to go there – they would take it so kindly if she should call on them. She had acted so often on his hints that he had formed a pleasant habit of expecting it: it made him feel so wisely responsible about giving them. But this one appeared to fall to the ground, so that he let the subject drop. Mrs. Alsager, however, went yet once more to the "Legitimate," as he found by her saying to him abruptly, on the morrow: "Oh, she'll be very good – she'll be very good." When they said "she," in these days, they always meant Violet Grey, though they pretended, for the most part, that they meant Nona Vincent.

"Oh yes," Wayworth assented, "she wants so to!"

Mrs. Alsager was silent a moment; then she asked, a little inconsequently, as if she had come back from a reverie: "Does she want to *very* much?"

"Tremendously – and it appears she has been fascinated by the part from the first."

"Why then didn't she say so?"

"Oh, because she's so funny."

"She *is* funny," said Mrs. Alsager, musingly; and presently she added: "She's in love with you."

Wayworth stared, blushed very red, then laughed out. "What is there funny in that?" he demanded; but before his interlocutress could satisfy him on this point he inquired, further, how she knew anything about it. After a little graceful evasion she explained that the night before, at the "Legitimate," Mrs. Beaumont, the wife of the actor-manager, had paid her a visit in her box; which had happened, in the course of their brief gossip, to lead to her remarking that she had never been "behind." Mrs. Beaumont offered on the spot to take her round, and the fancy had seized her to accept the invitation. She had been amused for the moment, and in this way it befell that her conductress, at her request, had introduced her to Miss Violet Grey, who was waiting in the wing for one of her scenes. Mrs. Beaumont had been called away for three minutes, and during this scrap of time, face to face with the actress, she had discovered the poor girl's secret. Wayworth qualified it as a senseless thing, but wished to know what had led to the discovery. She characterized this inquiry as superficial for a painter of the ways of women; and he doubtless didn't improve it by remarking profanely that a cat might look at a king and that such things were convenient to know. Even on this ground, however, he was threatened by Mrs. Alsager, who contended that it might not be a joking matter to the poor girl. To this Wayworth, who now professed to hate talking about the passions he might have inspired, could only reply that he meant it couldn't make a difference to Mrs. Alsager.

"How in the world do you know what makes a difference to *me?*" this lady asked, with incongruous coldness, with a haughtiness indeed remarkable in so gentle a spirit.

He saw Violet Grey that night at the theater, and it was she who spoke first of her having lately met a friend of his.

"She's in love with you," the actress said, after he had made a show of ignorance; "doesn't that tell you anything?"

He blushed redder still than Mrs. Alsager had made him blush, but replied, quickly enough and very adequately, that hundreds of women were naturally dying for him.

"Oh, I don't care, for you're not in love with *her!*" the girl continued.

"Did she tell you that too?" Wayworth asked; but she had at that moment to go on.

Standing where he could see her he thought that on this occasion she threw into her scene, which was the best she had in the play, a brighter art than ever before, a talent that could play with its problem. She was perpetually doing things out of rehearsal (she did two or three tonight, in the other man's piece), that he as often wished to heaven Nona Vincent might have the benefit of. She appeared to be able to do them for everyone but him – that is for everyone but Nona. He was conscious, in these days, of an odd new feeling, which mixed (this was a part of its oddity) with a very natural and comparatively old one and which in its most definite form was a dull ache of regret that this young lady's unlucky star should have placed her on the stage. He wished in his worst uneasiness that, without going further, she would give it up; and yet it soothed that uneasiness to remind himself that he saw grounds to hope she would go far enough to make a marked success of Nona. There were strange and painful moments when, as the interpretress of Nona, he almost hated her; after which, however, he always assured himself that he exaggerated, inasmuch as what made this aversion seem great, when he was nervous, was simply its contrast with the growing sense that there *were* grounds – totally different – on which she pleased him. She pleased him as a charming creature – by her sincerities and her perversities, by the varieties and surprises of her character and by certain happy facts of her person. In private her eyes were sad to him and her voice was rare. He detested the idea that she should have a disappointment or an humiliation, and he wanted to rescue her altogether, to save and transplant her. One way to save her was to see to it, to the best of his ability, that the production of his play should be a triumph; and the other way – it was really too queer to express – was almost to wish that it shouldn't be. Then, for the future, there would be safety and peace, and not the peace of death – the peace of a different life. It is to be added that our young man clung to the former of these ways in proportion as the latter perversely tempted him. He was nervous at the best, increasingly and intolerably nervous; but the immediate remedy was to rehearse harder and harder, and above all to work it out with Violet Grey. Some of her comrades reproached him with working it out only with her, as if she were the whole affair; to which he replied that they could afford to be neglected, they were all so tremendously good. She was the only person concerned whom he didn't flatter.

The author and the actress stuck so to the business in hand that she had very little time to speak to him again of Mrs. Alsager, of whom indeed her imagination appeared adequately to have disposed. Wayworth once remarked to her that Nona Vincent was supposed to be a good deal like his charming friend; but she gave a blank "Supposed by whom?" in consequence of which he never returned to the subject. He confided his nervousness as freely as usual to Mrs. Alsager, who easily understood that he had a peculiar complication of anxieties. His suspense varied in degree from hour to hour, but any relief there might have been in this was made up for by its being of several different kinds. One afternoon, as the first performance drew near, Mrs. Alsager said to him, in giving him his cup of tea and on his having mentioned that he had not closed his eyes the night before:

"You must indeed be in a dreadful state. Anxiety for another is still worse than anxiety for one's self."

"For another?" Wayworth repeated, looking at her over the rim of his cup.

"My poor friend, you're nervous about Nona Vincent, but you're infinitely more nervous about Violet Grey."

"She *is* Nona Vincent!"

"No, she isn't – not a bit!" said Mrs. Alsager, abruptly.

"Do you really think so?" Wayworth cried, spilling his tea in his alarm.

"What I think doesn't signify – I mean what I think about that. What I meant to say was that great as is your suspense about your play, your suspense about your actress is greater still."

"I can only repeat that my actress *is* my play."

Mrs. Alsager looked thoughtfully into the teapot.

"Your actress is your –"

"My what?" the young man asked, with a little tremor in his voice, as his hostess paused.

"Your very dear friend. You're in love with her – at present." And with a sharp click Mrs. Alsager dropped the lid on the fragrant receptacle.

"Not yet – not yet!" laughed her visitor.

"You will be if she pulls you through."

"You declare that she *won't* pull me through."

Mrs. Alsager was silent a moment, after which she softly murmured: "I'll pray for her."

"You're the most generous of women!" Wayworth cried; then colored as if the words had not been happy. They would have done indeed little honor to a man of tact.

The next morning he received five hurried lines from Mrs. Alsager. She had suddenly been called to Torquay, to see a relation who was seriously ill; she should be detained there several days, but she had an earnest hope of being able to return in time for his first night. In any event he had her unrestricted good wishes. He missed her extremely, for these last days were a great strain and there was little comfort to be derived from Violet Grey. She was even more nervous than himself, and so pale and altered that he was afraid she would be too ill to act. It was settled between them that they made each other worse and that he had now much better leave her alone. They had pulled Nona so to pieces that nothing seemed left of her – she must at least have time to grow together again. He left Violet Grey alone, to the best of his ability, but she carried out imperfectly her own side of the bargain. She came to him with new questions – she waited for him with old doubts, and half an hour before the last dress-rehearsal, on the eve of production, she proposed to him a totally fresh rendering of his heroine. This incident gave him such a sense of insecurity that he turned his back on her without a word, bolted out of the theater, dashed along the Strand and walked as far as the Bank. Then he jumped into a hansom and came westward, and when he reached the theater again the business was nearly over. It appeared, almost to his disappointment, not bad enough to give him the consolation of the old playhouse adage that the worst dress-rehearsals make the best first nights.

The morrow, which was a Wednesday, was the dreadful day; the theater had been closed on the Monday and the Tuesday. Everyone, on the Wednesday, did his best to let everyone else alone, and everyone signally failed in the attempt. The day, till seven o'clock, was understood to be consecrated to rest, but everyone except Violet Grey turned up at the theater. Wayworth looked at Mr. Loder, and Mr. Loder looked in another direction, which was as near as they came to conversation. Wayworth was in a fidget, unable to eat or sleep or sit still, at times almost in terror. He kept quiet by keeping, as usual, in motion; he tried to walk away from his nervousness. He walked in the afternoon toward Notting Hill, but he succeeded in not breaking the vow he had taken not to meddle with his actress. She was like an acrobat poised on a slippery ball – if he should touch her she would topple over. He passed her door three times and he thought of her three hundred. This was the hour at which he most regretted that Mrs. Alsager had not come back – for he had called at her house only to learn that she was still at Torquay. This was probably queer, and it was probably queerer still that she hadn't written to him; but even of these things he wasn't sure, for in losing, as he had now completely lost, his judgment of his play, he seemed to himself to have lost his judgment of everything. When he went home, however, he found a telegram from the lady of Grosvenor Place – "Shall be able to come – reach town by seven." At half-past eight o'clock, through a little aperture in the curtain of the "Renaissance," he saw her in her box with a cluster of friends – completely beautiful and beneficent. The house was magnificent – too good for his play, he felt; too good for any play. Everything now seemed too good – the scenery, the furniture, the dresses, the very programs. He seized upon the idea that this was probably what was the matter with the representative of Nona – she was only too good. He had completely arranged with this young lady the plan of their relations during the evening; and though they had altered everything else that they had arranged they had promised each other not to alter this. It was wonderful the number of things they had promised each other. He would start her, he would see her off – then he would quit the theater and stay away till just before the end. She besought him to stay away – it would make her infinitely easier. He saw that she was exquisitely dressed – she had made one or two changes for the better since the night before, and that seemed something definite to turn over and over in his mind as he rumbled foggily home in the four-wheeler in which, a few steps from the stage-door, he had taken refuge as soon as he knew that the curtain was up. He lived a couple of miles off, and he had chosen a four-wheeler to drag out the time.

When he got home his fire was out, his room was cold, and he lay down on his sofa in his overcoat. He had sent his landlady to the dress-circle, on purpose; she would overflow with words and mistakes. The house seemed a black void, just as the streets had done – everyone was, formidably, at his play. He was quieter at last than he had been for a fortnight, and he felt too weak even to wonder how the thing was going. He believed afterwards that he had slept an hour; but even if he had he felt it to be still too early to return to the theater. He sat down by his lamp and tried to read – to read a little compendious life of a great English statesman, out of a "series." It struck him as brilliantly clever, and he asked himself whether that perhaps were not rather the sort of thing he ought to have taken up: not the statesmanship, but the art of brief biography. Suddenly he became aware that he must hurry if he was to reach the theater at all – it was a quarter to eleven o'clock. He scrambled out and, this time, found a hansom – he had lately spent enough money in cabs to add to his hope that the profits of his new profession would be great. His anxiety, his suspense flamed up again, and as he rattled eastward – he went fast now – he was almost sick with alternations. As he passed into the theater the first man – some underling – who met him, cried to him, breathlessly:

"You're wanted, sir – you're wanted!" He thought his tone very ominous – he devoured the man's eyes with his own, for a betrayal: did he mean that he was wanted for execution? Someone else pressed him, almost pushed him, forward; he was already on the stage. Then he became conscious of a sound more or less continuous, but seemingly faint and far, which he took at first for the voice of the actors heard through their canvas walls, the beautiful built-in room of the last act. But the actors were in the wing, they surrounded him; the curtain was down and they were coming off from before it. They had been called, and *he* was called – they all greeted him with "Go on – go on!" He was terrified – he couldn't go on – he didn't believe in the applause, which seemed to him only audible enough to sound half-hearted.

"Has it gone? – *Has* it gone?" he gasped to the people round him; and he heard them say "Rather – rather!" perfunctorily, mendaciously too, as it struck him, and even with mocking laughter, the laughter of defeat and despair. Suddenly, though all this must have taken but a moment, Loder burst upon him from somewhere with a "For God's sake don't keep them, or they'll *stop!*" "But I can't go on for *that!*" Wayworth cried, in anguish; the sound seemed to him already to have ceased. Loder had hold of him and was shoving him; he resisted and looked round frantically for Violet Grey, who perhaps would tell him the truth. There was by this time a crowd in the wing, all with strange grimacing painted faces, but Violet was not among them and her very absence frightened him. He uttered her name with an accent that he afterwards regretted – it gave them, as he thought, both away; and while Loder hustled him before the curtain he heard someone say "She took her call and disappeared." She had had a call, then – this was what was most present to the young man as he stood for an instant in the glare of the footlights, looking blindly at the great vaguely-peopled horseshoe and greeted with plaudits which now seemed to him at once louder than he deserved and feebler than he desired. They sank to rest quickly, but he felt it to be long before he could back away, before he could, in his turn, seize the manager by the arm and cry huskily – "Has it really gone – *really?*"

Mr. Loder looked at him hard and replied after an instant: "The play's all right!"

Wayworth hung upon his lips. "Then what's all wrong?"

"We must do something to Miss Grey."

"What's the matter with her?"

"She isn't *in* it!"

"Do you mean she has failed?"

"Yes, damn it – she has failed."

Wayworth stared. "Then how can the play be all right?"

"Oh, we'll save it – we'll save it."

"Where's Miss Grey – where *is* she?" the young man asked.

Loder caught his arm as he was turning away again to look for his heroine. "Never mind her now – she knows it!"

Wayworth was approached at the same moment by a gentleman he knew as one of Mrs. Alsager's friends – he had perceived him in that lady's box. Mrs. Alsager was waiting there for the successful author; she desired very earnestly that he would come round and speak to her. Wayworth assured himself first that Violet had left the theater – one of the actresses could tell him that she had seen her throw on a cloak, without changing her dress, and had learnt afterwards that she had, the next moment, flung herself, after flinging her aunt, into a cab. He had wished to invite half a dozen persons, of whom Miss Grey and her elderly relative were two, to come home to supper with him; but she had refused to make any engagement beforehand (it would be so dreadful to have to keep it if she shouldn't have made a hit), and this attitude had blighted the pleasant plan, which fell to the ground. He had called her morbid, but she was immovable. Mrs. Alsager's messenger let him know that he was expected to supper in Grosvenor Place, and half an hour afterwards he was seated there among complimentary people and flowers and popping corks, eating the first orderly meal he had partaken of for a week. Mrs. Alsager had carried him off in her brougham – the other people who were coming got into things of their own. He stopped her short as soon as she began to tell him how tremendously everyone had been struck by the piece; he nailed her down to the question of Violet Grey. Had she spoilt the play, had she jeopardized or compromised it – had she been utterly bad, had she been good in any degree?

"Certainly the performance would have seemed better if *she* had been better," Mrs. Alsager confessed.

"And the play would have seemed better if the performance had been better," Wayworth said, gloomily, from the corner of the brougham.

"She does what she can, and she has talent, and she looked lovely. But she doesn't *see* Nona Vincent. She doesn't see the type – she doesn't see the individual – she doesn't see the woman you meant. She's out of it – she gives you a different person."

"Oh, the woman I meant!" the young man exclaimed, looking at the London lamps as he rolled by them. "I wish to God she had known *you!*" he added, as the carriage stopped. After they had passed into the house he said to his companion:

"You see she *won't* pull me through."

"Forgive her – be kind to her!" Mrs. Alsager pleaded.

"I shall only thank her. The play may go to the dogs."

"If it does – if it does," Mrs. Alsager began, with her pure eyes on him.

"Well, what if it does?"

She couldn't tell him, for the rest of her guests came in together; she only had time to say: "It *shan't* go to the dogs!"

He came away before the others, restless with the desire to go to Notting Hill even that night, late as it was, haunted with the sense that Violet Grey had measured her fall. When he got into the street, however, he allowed second thoughts to counsel another course; the effect of knocking her up at two o'clock in the morning would hardly be to soothe her. He looked at six newspapers the next day and found in them never a good word for her. They were well enough about the piece, but they were unanimous as to the disappointment caused by the young actress whose former efforts had excited such hopes and on whom, on this occasion, such pressing responsibilities rested. They asked in chorus what was the matter with her, and they declared in chorus that the play, which was not without promise, was handicapped (they all used the same word) by the odd want of correspondence between the heroine and her interpreter. Wayworth drove early to Notting Hill, but he didn't take the newspapers with him; Violet Grey could be trusted to have sent out for them by the peep of dawn and to have fed her anguish full. She declined to see him – she only sent down word by her aunt that she was extremely unwell and should be unable to act that night unless she were suffered to spend the day unmolested and in bed. Wayworth sat for an hour with the old lady, who understood everything and to whom he could speak frankly. She gave him a touching picture of her niece's condition, which was all the more vivid for the simple words in which it was expressed: "She feels she isn't right, you know – she feels she isn't right!"

"Tell her it doesn't matter – it doesn't matter a straw!" said Wayworth.

"And she's so proud – you know how proud she is!" the old lady went on.

"Tell her I'm more than satisfied, that I accept her gratefully as she is."

"She says she injures your play, that she ruins it," said his interlocutress.

"She'll improve, immensely – she'll grow into the part," the young man continued.

"She'd improve if she knew how – but she says she doesn't. She has given all she has got, and she doesn't know what's wanted."

"What's wanted is simply that she should go straight on and trust me."

"How can she trust you when she feels she's losing you?"

"Losing me?" Wayworth cried.

"You'll never forgive her if your play is taken off!"

"It will run six months," said the author of the piece.

The old lady laid her hand on his arm. "What will you do for her if it does?"

He looked at Violet Grey's aunt a moment. "Do you say your niece is very proud?"

"Too proud for her dreadful profession."

"Then she wouldn't wish you to ask me that," Wayworth answered, getting up.

When he reached home he was very tired, and for a person to whom it was open to consider that he had scored a success he spent a remarkably dismal day. All his restlessness had gone, and fatigue and depression possessed him. He sank into his old chair by the fire and sat there for hours with his eyes closed. His landlady came in to bring his luncheon and mend the fire, but he feigned to be asleep, so as not to be spoken to. It is to be supposed that sleep at last overtook him, for about the hour that dusk began to gather he had an extraordinary impression, a visit that, it would seem, could have belonged to no waking consciousness. Nona Vincent, in face and form, the living heroine of his play, rose before him in his little silent room, sat down with him at his dingy fireside. She was not Violet Grey, she was not Mrs. Alsager, she was not any woman he had seen upon earth, nor was it any masquerade of friendship or of penitence. Yet she was more familiar to him than the women he had known best, and she was ineffably beautiful and consoling. She filled the poor room with her presence, the effect of which was as soothing as some odor of incense. She was as quiet as an affectionate sister, and there was no surprise in her being there. Nothing more real had ever befallen him, and nothing, somehow, more reassuring. He felt her hand rest upon his own, and all his senses seemed to open to her message. She struck him, in the strangest way, both as his creation and as his inspirer, and she gave him the happiest consciousness of success. If she was so charming, in the red firelight, in her vague, clear-colored garments, it was because he had made her so, and yet if the weight seemed lifted from his spirit it was because she drew it away. When she bent her deep eyes upon him they seemed to speak of safety and freedom and to make a green garden of the future. From time to time she smiled and said: "I live – I live – I live." How long she stayed he couldn't have told, but when his landlady blundered in with the lamp Nona Vincent was no longer there. He rubbed his eyes, but no dream had ever been so intense; and as he slowly got out of his chair it was with a deep still joy

– the joy of the artist – in the thought of how right he had been, how exactly like herself he had made her. She had come to show him that. At the end of five minutes, however, he felt sufficiently mystified to call his landlady back – he wanted to ask her a question. When the good woman reappeared the question hung fire an instant; then it shaped itself as the inquiry:

"Has any lady been here?"

"No, sir – no lady at all."

The woman seemed slightly scandalized. "Not Miss Vincent?"

"Miss Vincent, sir?"

"The young lady of my play, don't you know?"

"Oh, sir, you mean Miss Violet Grey!"

"No I don't, at all. I think I mean Mrs. Alsager."

"There has been no Mrs. Alsager, sir."

"Nor anybody at all like her?"

The woman looked at him as if she wondered what had suddenly taken him. Then she asked in an injured tone: "Why shouldn't I have told you if you'd 'ad callers, sir?"

"I thought you might have thought I was asleep."

"Indeed you were, sir, when I came in with the lamp – and well you'd earned it, Mr. Wayworth!"

The landlady came back an hour later to bring him a telegram; it was just as he had begun to dress to dine at his club and go down to the theater.

"See me tonight in front, and don't come near me till it's over."

It was in these words that Violet communicated her wishes for the evening. He obeyed them to the letter; he watched her from the depths of a box. He was in no position to say how she might have struck him the night before, but what he saw during these charmed hours filled him with admiration and gratitude. She *was* in it, this time; she had pulled herself together, she had taken possession, she was felicitous at every turn. Fresh from his revelation of Nona he was in a position to judge, and as he judged he exulted. He was thrilled and carried away, and he was moreover intensely curious to know what had happened to her, by what unfathomable art she had managed in a few hours to effect such a change of base. It was as if *she* had had a revelation of Nona, so convincing a clearness had been breathed upon the picture. He kept himself quiet in the entr'actes – he would speak to her only at the end; but before the play was half over the manager burst into his box.

"It's prodigious, what she's up to!" cried Mr. Loder, almost more bewildered than gratified. "She has gone in for a new reading – a blessed somersault in the air!"

"Is it quite different?" Wayworth asked, sharing his mystification.

"Different? Hyperion to a satyr! It's devilish good, my boy!"

"It's devilish good," said Wayworth, "and it's in a different key altogether from the key of her rehearsal."

"I'll run you six months!" the manager declared; and he rushed round again to the actress, leaving Wayworth with a sense that she had already pulled him through. She had with the audience an immense personal success.

When he went behind, at the end, he had to wait for her; she only showed herself when she was ready to leave the theater. Her aunt had been in her dressing-room with her, and the two ladies appeared together. The girl passed him quickly, motioning him to say nothing till they should have got out of the place. He saw that she was immensely excited, lifted altogether above her common artistic level. The old lady said to him: "You must come home to supper with us: it has been all arranged." They had a brougham, with a little third seat, and he got into it with them. It was a long time before the actress would speak. She leaned back in her corner, giving no sign but still heaving a little, like a subsiding sea, and with all her triumph in the eyes that shone through the darkness. The old lady was hushed to awe, or at least to discretion, and Wayworth was happy enough to wait. He had really to wait till they had alighted at Notting Hill, where the elder of his companions went to see that supper had been attended to.

"I was better – I was better," said Violet Grey, throwing off her cloak in the little drawing room.

"You were perfection. You'll be like that every night, won't you?"

She smiled at him. "Every night? There can scarcely be a miracle every day."

"What do you mean by a miracle?"

"I've had a revelation."

Wayward stared. "At what hour?"

"The right hour – this afternoon. Just in time to save me – and to save *you.*"

"At five o'clock? Do you mean you had a visit?"

"She came to me – she stayed two hours."

"Two hours? Nona Vincent?"

"Mrs. Alsager." Violet Grey smiled more deeply. "It's the same thing."

"And how did Mrs. Alsager save you?"

"By letting me look at her. By letting me hear her speak. By letting me know her."

"And what did she say to you?"

"Kind things – encouraging, intelligent things."

"Ah, the dear woman!" Wayworth cried.

"You ought to like her – she likes *you.* She was just what I wanted," the actress added.

"Do you mean she talked to you about Nona?"

"She said you thought she was like her. She *is* – she's exquisite."

"She's exquisite," Wayworth repeated. "Do you mean she tried to coach you?"

"Oh, no – she only said she would be so glad if it would help me to see her. And I felt it did help me. I don't know what took place – she only sat there, and she held my hand and smiled at me, and she had tact and grace, and she had goodness and beauty, and she soothed my nerves and lighted up my imagination. Somehow she seemed to *give* it all to me. I took it – I took it. I kept her before me, I drank her in. For the first time, in the whole study of the part, I had my model – I could make my copy. All my courage came back to me, and other things came that I hadn't felt before. She was different – she was delightful; as I've said, she was a revelation. She kissed me when she went away – and you may guess if I kissed *her.* We were awfully affectionate, but it's *you* she likes!" said Violet Grey.

Wayworth had never been more interested in his life, and he had rarely been more mystified. "Did she wear vague, clear-colored garments?" he asked, after a moment.

Violet Grey stared, laughed, then bade him go in to supper. "*You* know how she dresses!"

He was very well pleased at supper, but he was silent and a little solemn. He said he would go to see Mrs. Alsager the next day. He did so, but he was told at her door that she had returned to Torquay. She remained there all winter, all spring, and the next time he saw her his play had run two hundred nights and he had married Violet Grey. His plays sometimes succeed, but his wife is not in them now, nor in any others. At these representations Mrs. Alsager continues frequently to be present.

The Chaperon

Chapter I

An old lady, in a high drawing room, had had her chair moved close to the fire, where she sat knitting and warming her knees. She was dressed in deep mourning; her face had a faded nobleness, tempered, however, by the somewhat illiberal compression assumed by her lips in obedience to something that was passing in her mind. She was far from the lamp, but though her eyes were fixed upon her active needles she was not looking at them. What she really saw was quite another train of affairs. The room was spacious and dim; the thick London fog had oozed into it even through its superior defenses. It was full of dusky, massive, valuable things. The old lady sat motionless save for the regularity of her clicking needles, which seemed as personal to her and as expressive as prolonged fingers. If she was thinking something out, she was thinking it thoroughly.

When she looked up, on the entrance of a girl of twenty, it might have been guessed that the appearance of this young lady was not an interruption of her meditation, but rather a contribution to it. The young lady, who was charming to behold, was also in deep mourning, which had a freshness, if mourning can be fresh, an air of having been lately put on. She went straight to the bell beside the chimneypiece and pulled it, while in her other hand she held a sealed and directed letter. Her companion glanced in silence at the letter; then she looked still harder at her work. The girl hovered near the fireplace, without speaking, and after a due, a dignified interval the butler appeared in response to the bell. The time had been sufficient to make the silence between the ladies seem long. The younger one asked the butler to see that her letter should be posted; and after he had gone out she moved vaguely about the room, as if to give her grandmother – for such was the elder personage – a chance to begin a colloquy of which she herself preferred not to strike the first note. As equally with herself her companion was on the face of it capable of holding out, the tension, though it was already late in the evening, might have lasted long. But the old lady after a little appeared to recognize, a trifle ungraciously, the girl's superior resources.

"Have you written to your mother?"

"Yes, but only a few lines, to tell her I shall come and see her in the morning."

"Is that all you've got to say?" asked the grandmother.

"I don't quite know what you want me to say."

"I want you to say that you've made up your mind."

"Yes, I've done that, granny."

"You intend to respect your father's wishes?"

"It depends upon what you mean by respecting them. I do justice to the feelings by which they were dictated."

"What do you mean by justice?" the old lady retorted.

The girl was silent a moment; then she said: "You'll see my idea of it."

"I see it already! You'll go and live with her."

"I shall talk the situation over with her tomorrow and tell her that I think that will be best."

"Best for her, no doubt!"

"What's best for her is best for me."

"And for your brother and sister?" As the girl made no reply to this her grandmother went on: "What's best for them is that you should acknowledge some responsibility in regard to them and, considering how young they are, try and do something for them."

"They must do as I've done – they must act for themselves. They have their means now, and they're free."

"Free? They're mere children."

"Let me remind you that Eric is older than I."

"He doesn't like his mother," said the old lady, as if that were an answer.

"I never said he did. And she adores him."

"Oh, your mother's adorations!"

"Don't abuse her now," the girl rejoined, after a pause.

The old lady forbore to abuse her, but she made up for it the next moment by saying: "It will be dreadful for Edith."

"What will be dreadful?"

"Your desertion of her."

"The desertion's on her side."

"Her consideration for her father does her honor."

"Of course I'm a brute, *n'en parlons plus,"* said the girl. "We must go our respective ways," she added, in a tone of extreme wisdom and philosophy.

Her grandmother straightened out her knitting and began to roll it up. "Be so good as to ring for my maid," she said, after a minute. The young lady rang, and there was another wait and another conscious hush. Before the maid came her mistress remarked: "Of course then you'll not come to *me,* you know."

"What do you mean by 'coming' to you?"

"I can't receive you on that footing."

"She'll not come *with* me, if you mean that."

"I don't mean that," said the old lady, getting up as her maid came in. This attendant took her work from her, gave her an arm and helped her out of the room, while Rose Tramore, standing before the fire and looking into it, faced the idea that her grandmother's door would now under all circumstances be closed to her. She lost no time however in brooding over this anomaly: it only added energy to her determination to act. All she could do tonight was to go to bed, for she felt utterly weary. She had been living, in imagination, in a prospective struggle, and it had left her as exhausted as a real fight. Moreover this was the culmination of a crisis, of weeks of suspense, of a long, hard strain. Her father had been laid in his grave five days before, and that morning his will had been read. In the afternoon she had got Edith off to St. Leonard's with their aunt Julia, and then she had had a wretched talk with Eric. Lastly, she had made up her mind to act in opposition to the formidable will, to a clause which embodied if not exactly a provision, a recommendation singularly emphatic. She went to bed and slept the sleep of the just.

"Oh, my dear, how charming! I must take another house!" It was in these words that her mother responded to the announcement Rose had just formally made and with which she had vaguely expected to produce a certain dignity of effect. In the way of emotion there was apparently no effect at all, and the girl was wise enough to know that this was not simply on account of the general line of non-allusion taken by the extremely pretty woman before her, who looked like her elder sister. Mrs. Tramore had never manifested, to her daughter, the slightest consciousness that her position was peculiar; but the recollection of something more than that fine policy was required to explain such a failure, to appreciate Rose's sacrifice. It was simply a fresh reminder that she had never appreciated anything, that she was nothing but a tinted and stippled surface. Her situation was peculiar indeed. She had been the heroine of a scandal which had grown dim only because, in the eyes of the London world, it paled in the lurid light of the contemporaneous. That attention had been fixed on it for several days, fifteen years before; there had been a high relish of the vivid evidence as to his wife's misconduct with which, in the divorce-court, Charles Tramore had judged well to regale a cynical public. The case was pronounced awfully bad, and he obtained his decree. The folly of the wife had been inconceivable, in spite of other examples: she had quitted her children, she had followed the "other fellow" abroad. The other fellow hadn't married her, not having had time: he had lost his life in the Mediterranean by the capsizing of a boat, before the prohibitory term had expired.

Mrs. Tramore had striven to extract from this accident something of the austerity of widowhood; but her mourning only made her deviation more public, she was a widow whose husband was awkwardly alive. She had not prowled about the Continent on the classic lines; she had come back to London to take her chance. But London would give her no chance, would have nothing to say to her; as many persons had remarked, you could never tell how London would behave. It would not receive Mrs. Tramore again on any terms, and when she was spoken of, which now was not often, it was inveterately said of her that she went nowhere. Apparently she had not the qualities for which London compounds; though in the cases in which it does compound you may often wonder what these qualities are. She had not at any rate been successful: her lover was dead, her husband was liked and her children were pitied, for in payment for a topic London will parenthetically pity. It was thought interesting and magnanimous that Charles Tramore had not married again. The disadvantage to his children of the miserable story was thus left uncorrected, and this, rather oddly, was counted as *his* sacrifice. His mother, whose arrangements were elaborate, looked after them a great deal, and they enjoyed a mixture of laxity and discipline under the roof of their aunt, Miss Tramore, who was independent, having, for reasons that the two ladies had exhaustively discussed, determined to lead her own life. She had set up a home at St. Leonard's, and that contracted shore had played a considerable part in the upbringing of the little Tramores. They knew about their mother, as the phrase was, but they didn't know her; which was naturally deemed more pathetic for them than for her. She had a house in Chester Square and an income and a victoria – it served all purposes, as she never went out in the evening – and flowers on her windowsills, and a remarkable appearance of youth. The income was supposed to be in part the result of a bequest from the man for whose sake she had committed the error of her life, and in the appearance of youth there was a slightly impertinent implication that it was a sort of afterglow of the same connection.

Her children, as they grew older, fortunately showed signs of some individuality of disposition. Edith, the second girl, clung to her aunt Julia; Eric, the son, clung frantically to polo; while Rose, the elder daughter, appeared to cling mainly to herself. Collectively, of course, they clung to their father, whose attitude in the family group, however, was casual and intermittent. He was charming and vague; he was like a clever actor who often didn't come to rehearsal. Fortune, which but for that one stroke had been generous to him, had provided him with deputies and trouble-takers, as well as with whimsical opinions, and a reputation for excellent taste, and whist at his club, and perpetual cigars on morocco sofas, and a beautiful absence of purpose. Nature had thrown in a remarkably fine hand, which he sometimes passed over his children's heads when they were glossy from the nursery brush. On Rose's eighteenth birthday he said to her that she might go to see her mother, on condition that her visits should be limited to an hour each time and to four in the year. She was to go alone; the other children were not included in the arrangement. This was the result of a visit that he himself had paid his repudiated wife at her urgent request, their only encounter during the fifteen years. The girl knew as much as this from her aunt Julia, who was full of tell-tale secrecies. She availed herself eagerly of the license, and in course of the period that elapsed before her father's death she spent with Mrs. Tramore exactly eight hours by the watch. Her father, who was as inconsistent and disappointing as he was amiable, spoke to her of her mother only once afterwards. This occasion had been the sequel of her first visit, and he had made no use of it to ask what she thought of the personality in Chester Square or how she liked it. He had only said "Did she take you out?" and when Rose answered "Yes, she put me straight into a carriage and drove me up and down Bond Street," had rejoined sharply "See that that never occurs again." It never did, but once was enough, everyone they knew having happened to be in Bond Street at that particular hour.

After this the periodical interview took place in private, in Mrs. Tramore's beautiful little wasted drawing room. Rose knew that, rare as these occasions were, her mother would not have kept her "all to herself" had there been anybody she could have shown her to. But in the poor lady's social void there was no one; she had after all her own correctness and she consistently preferred isolation to inferior contacts. So her daughter was subjected only to the maternal; it was not necessary to be definite in qualifying that. The girl had by this time a collection of ideas, gathered by impenetrable processes; she had tasted, in the ostracism of her ambiguous parent, of the acrid fruit of the tree of knowledge. She not only had an approximate vision of what everyone had done, but she had a private judgment for each case. She had a particular vision of her father, which did not interfere with his being dear to her, but which was directly concerned in her resolution, after his death, to do the special thing he had expressed the wish she should not do. In the general estimate her grandmother and her grandmother's money had their place, and the strong probability that any enjoyment of the latter commodity would now be withheld from her. It included Edith's marked inclination to receive the law, and doubtless eventually a more substantial memento, from Miss Tramore, and opened the question whether her own course might not contribute to make her sister's appear heartless. The answer to this question however would depend on the success that might attend her own, which would very possibly be small. Eric's attitude was eminently simple; he didn't care to know people who didn't know *his* people. If his mother should ever get back into society perhaps he would take her up. Rose Tramore had decided to do what she could to bring this consummation about; and strangely enough – so mixed were her superstitions and her heresies – a large part of her motive lay in the value she attached to such a consecration.

Of her mother intrinsically she thought very little now, and if her eyes were fixed on a special achievement it was much more for the sake of that achievement and to satisfy a latent energy that was in her than because her heart was wrung by this sufferer. Her heart had not been wrung at all, though she had quite held it out for the experience. Her purpose was a pious game, but it was still essentially a game. Among the ideas I have mentioned she had her idea of triumph. She had caught the inevitable note, the pitch, on her very first visit to Chester Square. She had arrived there in intense excitement, and her excitement was left on her hands in a manner that reminded her of a difficult air she had once heard sung at the opera when no one applauded the performer. That flatness had made her sick, and so did this, in another way. A part of her agitation proceeded from the fact that her aunt Julia had told her, in the manner of a burst of confidence, something she was not to repeat, that she was in appearance the very image of the lady in Chester Square. The motive that prompted this declaration was between aunt Julia and her conscience; but it was a great emotion to the girl to find her entertainer so beautiful. She was tall and exquisitely slim; she had hair more exactly to Rose Tramore's taste than any other she had ever seen, even to every detail in the way it was dressed, and a complexion and a figure of the kind that are always spoken of as "lovely." Her eyes were irresistible, and so were her clothes, though the clothes were perhaps a little more precisely the right thing than the eyes. Her appearance was marked to her daughter's sense by the highest distinction; though it may be mentioned that this had never been the opinion of all the world. It was a revelation to Rose that she herself might look a little like that. She knew however that aunt Julia had not seen her deposed sister-in-law for a long time, and she had a general impression that Mrs. Tramore was today a more complete production – for instance as regarded her air of youth – than she had ever been. There was no excitement on her side – that was all her visitor's; there was no emotion – that was excluded by the plan, to say nothing of conditions more primal. Rose had from the first a glimpse of her mother's plan. It was to mention nothing and imply nothing, neither to acknowledge, to explain nor to extenuate. She would leave everything to her child; with her child she was secure. She only wanted to get back into society; she would leave even that to her child, whom she treated not as a high-strung and heroic daughter, a creature of exaltation, of devotion, but as a new, charming, clever, useful friend, a little younger than herself. Already on that first day she had talked about dressmakers. Of course, poor thing, it was to be remembered that in her circumstances there were not many things she *could* talk about. "She wants to go out again; that's the only thing in the wide world she wants," Rose had promptly, compendiously said to herself. There had been a sequel to this observation, uttered, in intense engrossment, in her own room half an hour before she had, on the important evening, made known her decision to her grandmother: "Then I'll *take* her out!"

"She'll drag you down, she'll drag you down!" Julia Tramore permitted herself to remark to her niece, the next day, in a tone of feverish prophecy.

As the girl's own theory was that all the dragging there might be would be upward, and moreover administered by herself, she could look at her aunt with a cold and inscrutable eye.

"Very well, then, I shall be out of your sight, from the pinnacle you occupy, and I shan't trouble you."

"Do you reproach me for my disinterested exertions, for the way I've toiled over you, the way I've lived for you?" Miss Tramore demanded.

"Don't reproach *me* for being kind to my mother and I won't reproach you for anything."

"She'll keep you out of everything – she'll make you miss everything," Miss Tramore continued.

"Then she'll make me miss a great deal that's odious," said the girl.

"You're too young for such extravagances," her aunt declared.

"And yet Edith, who is younger than I, seems to be too old for them: how do you arrange that? My mother's society will make me older," Rose replied.

"Don't speak to me of your mother; you *have* no mother."

"Then if I'm an orphan I must settle things for myself."

"Do you justify her, do you approve of her?" cried Miss Tramore, who was inferior to her niece in capacity for retort and whose limitations made the girl appear pert.

Rose looked at her a moment in silence; then she said, turning away: "I think she's charming."

"And do you propose to become charming in the same manner?"

"Her manner is perfect; it would be an excellent model. But I can't discuss my mother with you."

"You'll have to discuss her with some other people!" Miss Tramore proclaimed, going out of the room.

Rose wondered whether this were a general or a particular vaticination. There was something her aunt might have meant by it, but her aunt rarely meant the best thing she might have meant. Miss Tramore had come up from St. Leonard's in response to a telegram from her own parent, for an occasion like the present brought with it, for a few hours, a certain relaxation of their dissent. "Do what you can to stop her," the old lady had said; but her daughter found that the most she could do was not much. They both had a baffled sense that Rose had thought the question out a good deal further than they; and this was particularly irritating to Mrs. Tramore, as consciously the cleverer of the two. A question thought out as far as *she* could think it had always appeared to her to have performed its human uses; she had never encountered a ghost emerging from that extinction. Their great contention was that Rose would cut herself off; and certainly if she wasn't afraid of that she wasn't afraid of anything. Julia Tramore could only tell her mother how little the girl was afraid. She was already prepared to leave the house, taking with her the possessions, or her share of them, that had accumulated there during her father's illness. There had been a going and coming of her maid, a thumping about of boxes, an ordering of four-wheelers; it appeared to old Mrs. Tramore that something of the objectionableness, the indecency, of her granddaughter's prospective connection had already gathered about the place. It was a violation of the decorum of bereavement which was still fresh there, and from the indignant gloom of the mistress of the house you might have inferred not so much that the daughter was about to depart as that the mother was about to arrive. There had been no conversation on the dreadful subject at luncheon; for at luncheon at Mrs. Tramore's (her son never came to it) there were always, even after funerals and other miseries, stray guests of both sexes whose policy it was to be cheerful and superficial. Rose had sat down as if nothing had happened – nothing worse, that is, than her father's death; but no one had spoken of anything that anyone else was thinking of.

Before she left the house a servant brought her a message from her grandmother – the old lady desired to see her in the drawing room. She had on her bonnet, and she went down as if she were about to step into her cab. Mrs. Tramore sat there with her eternal knitting, from which she forbore even to raise her eyes as, after a silence that seemed to express the fullness of her reprobation, while Rose stood motionless, she began: "I wonder if you really understand what you're doing."

"I think so. I'm not so stupid."

"I never thought you were; but I don't know what to make of you now. You're giving up everything."

The girl was tempted to inquire whether her grandmother called herself "everything"; but she checked this question, answering instead that she knew she was giving up much.

"You're taking a step of which you will feel the effect to the end of your days," Mrs. Tramore went on.

"In a good conscience, I heartily hope," said Rose.

"Your father's conscience was good enough for his mother; it ought to be good enough for his daughter."

Rose sat down – she could afford to – as if she wished to be very attentive and were still accessible to argument. But this demonstration only ushered in, after a moment, the surprising words "I don't think papa had any conscience."

"What in the name of all that's unnatural do you mean?" Mrs. Tramore cried, over her glasses. "The dearest and best creature that ever lived!"

"He was kind, he had charming impulses, he was delightful. But he never reflected."

Mrs. Tramore stared, as if at a language she had never heard, a farrago, a galimatias. Her life was made up of items, but she had never had to deal, intellectually, with a fine shade. Then while her needles, which had paused an instant, began to fly again, she rejoined: "Do you know what you are, my dear? You're a dreadful little prig. Where do you pick up such talk?"

"Of course I don't mean to judge between them," Rose pursued. "I can only judge between my mother and myself. Papa couldn't judge for me." And with this she got up.

"One would think you were horrid. I never thought so before."

"Thank you for that."

"You're embarking on a struggle with society," continued Mrs. Tramore, indulging in an unusual flight of oratory. "Society will put you in your place."

"Hasn't it too many other things to do?" asked the girl.

This question had an ingenuity which led her grandmother to meet it with a merely provisional and somewhat sketchy answer. "Your ignorance would be melancholy if your behavior were not so insane."

"Oh, no; I know perfectly what she'll do!" Rose replied, almost gaily. "She'll drag me down."

"She won't even do that," the old lady declared contradictiously. "She'll keep you forever in the same dull hole."

"I shall come and see *you,* granny, when I want something more lively."

"You may come if you like, but you'll come no further than the door. If you leave this house now you don't enter it again."

Rose hesitated a moment. "Do you really mean that?"

"You may judge whether I choose such a time to joke."

"Good-bye, then," said the girl.

"Good-bye."

Rose quitted the room successfully enough; but on the other side of the door, on the landing, she sank into a chair and buried her face in her hands. She had burst into tears, and she sobbed there for a moment, trying hard to recover herself, so as to go downstairs without showing any traces of emotion, passing before the servants and again perhaps before aunt Julia. Mrs. Tramore was too old to cry; she could only drop her knitting and, for a long time, sit with her head bowed and her eyes closed.

Rose had reckoned justly with her aunt Julia; there were no footmen, but this vigilant virgin was posted at the foot of the stairs. She offered no challenge however; she only said: "There's someone in the parlor who wants to see you." The girl demanded a name, but Miss Tramore only mouthed inaudibly and winked and waved. Rose instantly reflected that there was only one man in the world her aunt would look such deep things about. "Captain Jay?" her own eyes asked, while Miss Tramore's were those of a conspirator: they were, for a moment, the only embarrassed eyes Rose had encountered that day. They contributed to make aunt Julia's further response evasive, after her niece inquired if she had communicated in advance with this visitor. Miss Tramore merely said that he had been upstairs with her mother – hadn't she mentioned it? – and had been waiting for her. She thought herself acute in not putting the question of the girl's seeing him before her as a favor to him or to herself; she presented it as a duty, and wound up with the proposition: "It's not fair to him, it's not kind, not to let him speak to you before you go."

"What does he want to say?" Rose demanded.

"Go in and find out."

She really knew, for she had found out before; but after standing uncertain an instant she went in. "The parlor" was the name that had always been borne by a spacious sitting room downstairs, an apartment occupied by her father during his frequent phases of residence in Hill Street – episodes increasingly frequent after his house in the country had, in consequence, as Rose perfectly knew, of his spending too much money, been disposed of at a sacrifice which he always characterized as horrid. He had been left with the place in Hertfordshire and his mother with the London house, on the general understanding that they would change about; but during the last years the community had grown more rigid, mainly at his mother's expense. The parlor was full of his memory and his habits and his things – his books and pictures and bibelots, objects that belonged now to Eric. Rose had sat in it for hours since his death; it was the place in which she could still be nearest to him. But she felt far from him as Captain Jay rose erect on her opening the door. This was a very different presence. He had not liked Captain Jay. She herself had, but not enough to make a great complication of her father's coldness. This afternoon however she foresaw complications. At the very outset for instance she was not pleased with his having arranged such a surprise for her with her grandmother and her aunt. It was probably aunt Julia who had sent for him; her grandmother wouldn't have done it. It placed him immediately on their side, and Rose was almost as disappointed at this as if she had not known it was quite where he would naturally be. He had never paid her a special visit, but if that was what he wished to do why shouldn't he have waited till she should be under her mother's roof? She knew the reason, but she had an angry prospect of enjoyment in making him express it. She liked him enough, after all, if it were measured by the idea of what she could make him do.

In Bertram Jay the elements were surprisingly mingled; you would have gone astray, in reading him, if you had counted on finding the complements of some of his qualities. He would not however have struck you in the least as incomplete, for in every case in which you didn't find the complement you would have found the contradiction. He was in the Royal Engineers, and was tall, lean and high-shouldered. He looked every inch a soldier, yet there were people who considered that he had missed his vocation in not becoming a parson. He took a public interest in the spiritual life of the army. Other persons still, on closer observation, would have felt that his most appropriate field was neither the army nor the church, but simply the world – the social, successful, worldly world. If he had a sword in one hand and a Bible in the other he had a Court Guide concealed somewhere about his person. His profile was hard and handsome, his eyes were both cold and kind, his dark straight hair was imperturbably smooth and prematurely streaked with grey. There was nothing in existence that he didn't take seriously. He had a first-rate power of work and an ambition as minutely organized as a German plan of invasion. His only real recreation was to go to church, but he went to parties when he had time. If he was in love with Rose Tramore this was distracting to him only in the same sense as his religion, and it was included in that department of his extremely sub-divided life. His religion indeed was of an encroaching, annexing sort. Seen from in front he looked diffident and blank, but he was capable of exposing himself in a way (to speak only of the paths of peace) wholly inconsistent with shyness. He had a passion for instance for open-air speaking, but was not thought on the whole to excel in it unless he could help himself out with a hymn. In conversation he kept his eyes on you with a kind of colorless candor, as if he had not understood what you were saying and, in a fashion that made many people turn red, waited before answering. This was only because he was considering their remarks in more relations than they had intended. He had in his face no expression whatever save the one just mentioned, and was, in his profession, already very distinguished.

He had seen Rose Tramore for the first time on a Sunday of the previous March, at a house in the country at which she was staying with her father, and five weeks later he had made her, by letter, an offer of marriage. She showed her father the letter of course, and he told her that it would give him great pleasure that she should send Captain Jay about his business. "My dear child," he said, "we must really have someone who will be better fun than that." Rose had declined the honor, very considerately and kindly, but not simply because her father wished it. She didn't herself wish to detach this flower from the stem, though when the young man wrote again, to express the hope that he *might* hope – so long was he willing to wait – and ask if he might not still sometimes see her, she answered even more indulgently than at first. She had shown her father her former letter, but she didn't show him this one; she only told him what it contained, submitting to him also that of her correspondent. Captain Jay moreover wrote to Mr. Tramore, who replied sociably, but so vaguely that he almost neglected the subject under discussion – a communication that made poor Bertram ponder long. He could never get to the bottom of the superficial, and all the proprieties and conventions of life were profound to him. Fortunately for him old Mrs. Tramore liked him, he was satisfactory to her long-sightedness; so that a relation was established under cover of which he still occasionally presented himself in Hill Street – presented himself nominally to the mistress of the house. He had had scruples about the veracity of his visits, but he had disposed of them; he had scruples about so many things that he had had to invent a general way, to dig a central drain. Julia Tramore happened to meet him when she came up to town, and she took a view of him more benevolent than her usual estimate of people encouraged by her mother. The fear of agreeing with that lady was a motive, but there was a stronger one, in this particular case, in the fear of agreeing with her niece, who had rejected him. His situation might be held to have improved when Mr. Tramore was taken so gravely ill that with regard to his recovery those about him left their eyes to speak for their lips; and in the light of the poor gentleman's recent death it was doubtless better than it had ever been.

He was only a quarter of an hour with the girl, but this gave him time to take the measure of it. After he had spoken to her about her bereavement, very much as an especially mild missionary might have spoken to a beautiful Polynesian, he let her know that he had learned from her companions the very strong step she was about to take. This led to their spending together ten minutes which, to her mind, threw more light on his character than anything that had ever passed between them. She had always felt with him as if she were standing on an edge, looking down into something decidedly deep. Today the impression of the perpendicular shaft was there, but it was rather an abyss of confusion and disorder than the large bright space in which she had figured everything as ranged and pigeon-holed, presenting the appearance of the labeled shelves and drawers at a chemist's. He discussed without an invitation to discuss, he appealed without a right to appeal. He was nothing but a suitor tolerated after dismissal, but he took strangely for granted a participation in her affairs. He assumed all sorts of things that made her draw back. He implied that there was everything now to assist them in arriving at an agreement, since she had never informed him that he was positively objectionable; but that this symmetry would be spoiled if she should not be willing to take a little longer to think of certain consequences. She was greatly disconcerted when she saw what consequences he meant and at his reminding her of them. What on earth was the use of a lover if he was to speak only like one's grandmother and one's aunt? He struck her as much in love with her and as particularly careful at the same time as to what he might say. He never mentioned her mother; he only alluded, indirectly but earnestly, to the "step." He disapproved of it altogether, took an unexpectedly prudent, politic view of it. He evidently also believed that she would be dragged down; in other words that she would not be asked out. It was his idea that her mother would contaminate her, so that he should find himself interested in a young person discredited and virtually unmarriageable. All this was more obvious to him than the consideration that a daughter should be merciful. Where was his religion if he understood mercy so little, and where were his talent and his courage if he were so miserably afraid of trumpery social penalties? Rose's heart sank when she reflected that a man supposed to be first-rate hadn't guessed that rather than not do what she could for her mother she would give up all the Engineers in the world. She became aware that she probably would have been moved to place her hand in his on the spot if he had come to her saying "Your idea is the right one; put it through at every cost." She couldn't discuss this with him, though he impressed her as having too much at stake for her to treat him with mere disdain. She sickened at the revelation that a gentleman could see so much in mere vulgarities of opinion, and though she uttered as few words as possible, conversing only in sad smiles and headshakes and in intercepted movements toward the door, she happened, in some unguarded lapse from her reticence, to use the expression that she was disappointed in him. He caught at it and, seeming to drop his field-glass, pressed upon her with nearer, tenderer eyes.

"Can I be so happy as to believe, then, that you had thought of me with some confidence, with some faith?"

"If you didn't suppose so, what is the sense of this visit?" Rose asked.

"One can be faithful without reciprocity," said the young man. "I regard you in a light which makes me want to protect you even if I have nothing to gain by it."

"Yet you speak as if you thought you might keep me for yourself."

"For *yourself.* I don't want you to suffer."

"Nor to suffer yourself by my doing so," said Rose, looking down.

"Ah, if you would only marry me next month!" he broke out inconsequently.

"And give up going to mamma?" Rose waited to see if he would say "What need that matter? Can't your mother come to us?" But he said nothing of the sort; he only answered -

"She surely would be sorry to interfere with the exercise of any other affection which I might have the bliss of believing that you are now free, in however small a degree, to entertain."

Rose knew that her mother wouldn't be sorry at all; but she contented herself with rejoining, her hand on the door: "Good-bye. I shan't suffer. I'm not afraid."

"You don't know how terrible, how cruel, the world can be."

"Yes, I do know. I know everything!"

The declaration sprang from her lips in a tone which made him look at her as he had never looked before, as if he saw something new in her face, as if he had never yet known her. He hadn't displeased her so much but that she would like to give him that impression, and since she felt that she was doing so she lingered an instant for the purpose. It enabled her to see, further, that he turned red; then to become aware that a carriage had stopped at the door. Captain Jay's eyes, from where he stood, fell upon this arrival, and the nature of their glance made Rose step forward to look. Her mother sat there, brilliant, conspicuous, in the eternal victoria, and the footman was already sounding the knocker. It had been no part of the arrangement that she should come to fetch her; it had been out of the question – a stroke in such bad taste as would have put Rose in the wrong. The girl had never dreamed of it, but somehow, suddenly, perversely, she was glad of it now; she even hoped that her grandmother and her aunt were looking out upstairs.

"My mother has come for me. Good-bye," she repeated; but this time her visitor had got between her and the door.

"Listen to me before you go. I will give you a life's devotion," the young man pleaded. He really barred the way.

She wondered whether her grandmother had told him that if her flight were not prevented she would forfeit money. Then, vividly, it came over her that this would be what he was occupied with. "I shall never think of you – let me go!" she cried, with passion.

Captain Jay opened the door, but Rose didn't see his face, and in a moment she was out of the house. Aunt Julia, who was sure to have been hovering, had taken flight before the profanity of the knock.

"Heavens, dear, where did you get your mourning?" the lady in the victoria asked of her daughter as they drove away.

Chapter II

Lady Maresfield had given her boy a push in his plump back and had said to him, "Go and speak to her now; it's your chance." She had for a long time wanted this scion to make himself audible to Rose Tramore, but the opportunity was not easy to come by. The case was complicated. Lady Maresfield had four daughters, of whom only one was married. It so happened moreover that this one, Mrs. Vaughan-Vesey, the only person in the world her mother was afraid of, was the most to be reckoned with. The Honorable Guy was in appearance all his mother's child, though he was really a simpler soul. He was large and pink; large, that is, as to everything but the eyes, which were diminishing points, and pink as to everything but the hair, which was comparable, faintly, to the hue of the richer rose. He had also, it must be conceded, very small neat teeth, which made his smile look like a young lady's. He had no wish to resemble any such person, but he was perpetually smiling, and he smiled more than ever as he approached Rose Tramore, who, looking altogether, to his mind, as a pretty girl should, and wearing a soft white opera-cloak over a softer black dress, leaned alone against the wall of the vestibule at Covent Garden while, a few paces off, an old gentleman engaged her mother in conversation. Madame Patti had been singing, and they were all waiting for their carriages. To their ears at present came a vociferation of names and a rattle of wheels. The air, through banging doors, entered in damp, warm gusts, heavy with the stale, slightly sweet taste of the London season when the London season is overripe and spoiling.

Guy Mangler had only three minutes to reestablish an interrupted acquaintance with our young lady. He reminded her that he had danced with her the year before, and he mentioned that he knew her brother. His mother had lately been to see old Mrs. Tramore, but this he did not mention, not being aware of it. That visit had produced, on Lady Maresfield's part, a private crisis, engendered ideas. One of them was that the grandmother in Hill Street had really forgiven the willful girl much more than she admitted. Another was that there would still be some money for Rose when the others should come into theirs. Still another was that the others would come into theirs at no distant date; the old lady was so visibly going to pieces. There were several more besides, as for instance that Rose had already fifteen hundred a year from her father. The figure had been betrayed in Hill Street; it was part of the proof of Mrs. Tramore's decrepitude. Then there was an equal amount that her mother had to dispose of and on which the girl could absolutely count, though of course it might involve much waiting, as the mother, a person of gross insensibility, evidently wouldn't die of cold-shouldering. Equally definite, to do it justice, was the conception that Rose was in truth remarkably good looking, and that what she had undertaken to do showed, and would show even should it fail, cleverness of the right sort. Cleverness of the right sort was exactly the quality that Lady Maresfield prefigured as indispensable in a young lady to whom she should marry her second son, over whose own deficiencies she flung the veil of a maternal theory that *his* cleverness was of a sort that was wrong. Those who knew him less well were content to wish that he might not conceal it for such a scruple. This enumeration of his mother's views does not exhaust the list, and it was in obedience to one too profound to be uttered even by the historian that, after a very brief delay, she decided to move across the crowded lobby. Her daughter Bessie was the only one with her; Maggie was dining with the Vaughan-Veseys, and Fanny was not of an age. Mrs. Tramore the younger showed only an admirable back – her face was to her old gentleman – and Bessie had drifted to some other people; so that it was comparatively easy for Lady Maresfield to say to Rose, in a moment: "My dear child, are you never coming to see us?"

"We shall be delighted to come if you'll ask us," Rose smiled.

Lady Maresfield had been prepared for the plural number, and she was a woman whom it took many plurals to disconcert. "I'm sure Guy is longing for another dance with you," she rejoined, with the most unblinking irrelevance.

"I'm afraid we're not dancing again quite yet," said Rose, glancing at her mother's exposed shoulders, but speaking as if they were muffled in crape.

Lady Maresfield leaned her head on one side and seemed almost wistful. "Not even at my sister's ball? She's to have something next week. She'll write to you."

Rose Tramore, on the spot, looking bright but vague, turned three or four things over in her mind. She remembered that the sister of her interlocutress was the proverbially rich Mrs. Bray, a bankeress or a breweress or a builderess, who had so big a house that she couldn't fill it unless she opened her doors, or her mouth, very wide. Rose had learnt more about London society during these lonely months with her mother than she had ever picked up in Hill Street. The younger Mrs. Tramore was a mine of commerages, and she had no need to go out to bring home the latest intelligence. At any rate Mrs. Bray might serve as the end of a wedge. "Oh, I dare say we might think of that," Rose said. "It would be very kind of your sister."

"Guy'll think of it, won't you, Guy?" asked Lady Maresfield.

"Rather!" Guy responded, with an intonation as fine as if he had learnt it at a music hall; while at the same moment the name of his mother's carriage was bawled through the place. Mrs. Tramore had parted with her old gentleman; she turned again to her daughter.

Nothing occurred but what always occurred, which was exactly this absence of everything – a universal lapse. She didn't exist, even for a second, to any recognizing eye. The people who looked at her – of course there were plenty of those – were only the people who didn't exist for hers. Lady Maresfield surged away on her son's arm.

It was this noble matron herself who wrote, the next day, enclosing a card of invitation from Mrs. Bray and expressing the hope that Rose would come and dine and let her ladyship take her. She should have only one of her own girls; Gwendolen Vesey was to take the other. Rose handed both the note and the card in silence to her mother; the latter exhibited only the name of Miss Tramore. "You had much better go, dear," her mother said; in answer to which Miss Tramore slowly tore up the documents, looking with clear, meditative eyes out of the window. Her mother always said "You had better go" – there had been other incidents – and Rose had never even once taken account of the observation. She would make no first advances, only plenty of second ones, and, condoning no discrimination, would treat no omission as venial. She would keep all concessions till afterwards; then she would make them one by one. Fighting society was quite as hard as her grandmother had said it would be; but there was a tension in it which made the dreariness vibrate – the dreariness of such a winter as she had just passed. Her companion had cried at the end of it, and she had cried all through; only her tears had been private, while her mother's had fallen once for all, at luncheon on the bleak Easter Monday – produced by the way a silent survey of the deadly square brought home to her that every creature but themselves was out of town and having tremendous fun. Rose felt that it was useless to attempt to explain simply by her mourning this severity of solitude; for if people didn't go to parties (at least a few didn't) for six months after their father died, this was the very time other people took for coming to see them. It was not too much to say that during this first winter of Rose's period with her mother she had no communication whatever with the world. It had the effect of making her take to reading the new American books: she wanted to see how girls got on by themselves. She had never read so much before, and there was a legitimate indifference in it when topics failed with her mother. They often failed after the first days, and then, while she bent over instructive volumes, this lady, dressed as if for an impending function, sat on the sofa and watched her. Rose was not embarrassed by such an appearance, for she could reflect that, a little before, her companion had not even a girl who had taken refuge in queer researches to look at. She was moreover used to her mother's attitude by this time. She had her own description of it: it was the attitude of waiting for the carriage. If they didn't go out it was not that Mrs. Tramore was not ready in time, and Rose had even an alarmed prevision of their some day always arriving first. Mrs. Tramore's conversation at such moments was abrupt, inconsequent and personal. She sat on the edge of sofas and chairs and glanced occasionally at the fit of her gloves (she was perpetually gloved, and the fit was a thing it was melancholy to see wasted), as people do who are expecting guests to dinner. Rose used almost to fancy herself at times a perfunctory husband on the other side of the fire.

What she was not yet used to – there was still a charm in it – was her mother's extraordinary tact. During the years they lived together they never had a discussion; a circumstance all the more remarkable since if the girl had a reason for sparing her companion (that of being sorry for her) Mrs. Tramore had none for sparing her child. She only showed in doing so a happy instinct – the happiest thing about her. She took in perfection a course which represented everything and covered everything; she utterly abjured all authority. She testified to her abjuration in hourly ingenious, touching ways. In this manner nothing had to be talked over, which was a mercy all round. The tears on Easter Monday were merely a nervous gust, to help show she was not a Christmas doll from the Burlington Arcade; and there was no lifting up of the repentant Magdalen, no uttered remorse for the former abandonment of children. Of the way she could treat her children her demeanor to this one was an example; it was an uninterrupted appeal to her eldest daughter for direction. She took the law from Rose in every circumstance, and if you had noticed these ladies without knowing their history you would have wondered what tie was fine enough to make maturity so respectful to youth. No mother was ever so filial as Mrs. Tramore, and there had never been such a difference of position between sisters. Not that the elder one fawned, which would have been fearful; she only renounced – whatever she had to renounce. If the amount was not much she at any rate made no scene over it. Her hand was so light that Rose said of her secretly, in vague glances at the past, "No wonder people liked her!" She never characterized the old element of interference with her mother's respectability more definitely than as "people." They were people, it was true, for whom gentleness must have been everything and who didn't demand a variety of interests. The desire to "go out" was the one passion that even a closer acquaintance with her parent revealed to Rose Tramore. She marveled at its strength, in the light of the poor lady's history: there was comedy enough in this unquenchable flame on the part of a woman who had known such misery. She had drunk deep of every dishonor, but the bitter cup had left her with a taste for lighted candles, for squeezing up staircases and hooking herself to the human elbow. Rose had a vision of the future years in which this taste would grow with restored exercise – of her mother, in a long-tailed dress, jogging on and on and on, jogging further and further from her sins, through a century of the "Morning Post" and down the fashionable avenue of time. She herself would then be very old – she herself would be dead. Mrs. Tramore would cover a span of life for which such an allowance of sin was small. The girl could laugh indeed now at that theory of her being dragged down. If one thing were more present to her than another it was the very desolation of their propriety. As she glanced at her companion, it sometimes seemed to her that if she had been a bad woman she would have been worse than that. There were compensations for being "cut" which Mrs. Tramore too much neglected.

The lonely old lady in Hill Street – Rose thought of her that way now – was the one person to whom she was ready to say that she would come to her on any terms. She wrote this to her three times over, and she knocked still oftener at her door. But the old lady answered no letters; if Rose had remained in Hill Street it would have been her own function to answer them; and at the door, the butler, whom the girl had known for ten years, considered her, when he told her his mistress was not at home, quite as he might have considered a young person who had come about a place and of whose eligibility he took a negative view. That was Rose's one pang, that she probably appeared rather heartless. Her aunt Julia had gone to Florence with Edith for the winter, on purpose to make her appear more so; for Miss Tramore was still the person most scandalized by her secession. Edith and she, doubtless, often talked over in Florence the destitution of the aged victim in Hill Street. Eric never came to see his sister, because, being full both of family and of personal feeling, he thought she really ought to have stayed with his grandmother. If she had had such an appurtenance all to herself she might have done what she liked with it; but he couldn't forgive such a want of consideration for anything of his. There were moments when Rose would have been ready to take her hand from the plow and insist upon reintegration, if only the fierce voice of the old house had allowed people to look her up. But she read, ever so clearly, that her grandmother had made this a question of loyalty to seventy years of virtue. Mrs. Tramore's forlornness didn't prevent her drawing room from being a very public place, in which Rose could hear certain words reverberate: "Leave her alone; it's the only way to see how long she'll hold out." The old woman's visitors were people who didn't wish to quarrel, and the girl was conscious that if they had not let her alone – that is if they had come to her from her grandmother – she might perhaps not have held out. She had no friends quite of her own; she had not been brought up to have them, and it would not have been easy in a house which two such persons as her father and his mother divided between them. Her father disapproved of crude intimacies, and all the intimacies of youth were crude. He had married at five-and-twenty and could testify to such a truth. Rose felt that she shared even Captain Jay with her grandmother; she had seen what *he* was worth. Moreover, she had spoken to him at that last moment in Hill Street in a way which, taken with her former refusal, made it impossible that he should come near her again. She hoped he went to see his protectress: he could be a kind of substitute and administer comfort.

It so happened, however, that the day after she threw Lady Maresfield's invitation into the wastepaper basket she received a visit from a certain Mrs. Donovan, whom she had occasionally seen in Hill Street. She vaguely knew this lady for a busybody, but she was in a situation which even busybodies might alleviate. Mrs. Donovan was poor, but honest – so scrupulously honest that she was perpetually returning visits she had never received. She was always clad in weather-beaten sealskin, and had an odd air of being prepared for the worst, which was borne out by her denying that she was Irish. She was of the English Donovans.

"Dear child, won't you go out with me?" she asked.

Rose looked at her a moment and then rang the bell. She spoke of something else, without answering the question, and when the servant came she said: "Please tell Mrs. Tramore that Mrs. Donovan has come to see her."

"Oh, that'll be delightful; only you mustn't tell your grandmother!" the visitor exclaimed.

"Tell her what?"

"That I come to see your mamma."

"You don't," said Rose.

"Sure I hoped you'd introduce me!" cried Mrs. Donovan, compromising herself in her embarrassment.

"It's not necessary; you knew her once."

"Indeed and I've known everyone once," the visitor confessed.

Mrs. Tramore, when she came in, was charming and exactly right; she greeted Mrs. Donovan as if she had met her the week before last, giving her daughter such a new illustration of her tact that Rose again had the idea that it was no wonder "people" had liked her. The girl grudged Mrs. Donovan so fresh a morsel as a description of her mother at home, rejoicing that she would be inconvenienced by having to keep the story out of Hill Street. Her mother went away before Mrs. Donovan departed, and Rose was touched by guessing her reason – the thought that since even this circuitous personage had been moved to come, the two might, if left together, invent some remedy. Rose waited to see what Mrs. Donovan had in fact invented.

"You won't come out with me then?"

"Come out with you?"

"My daughters are married. You know I'm a lone woman. It would be an immense pleasure to me to have so charming a creature as yourself to present to the world."

"I go out with my mother," said Rose, after a moment.

"Yes, but sometimes when she's not inclined?"

"She goes everywhere she wants to go," Rose continued, uttering the biggest fib of her life and only regretting it should be wasted on Mrs. Donovan.

"Ah, but do you go everywhere *you* want?" the lady asked sociably.

"One goes even to places one hates. Everyone does that."

"Oh, what I go through!" this social martyr cried. Then she laid a persuasive hand on the girl's arm. "Let me show you at a few places first, and then we'll see. I'll bring them all here."

"I don't think I understand you," replied Rose, though in Mrs. Donovan's words she perfectly saw her own theory of the case reflected. For a quarter of a minute she asked herself whether she might not, after all, do so much evil that good might come. Mrs. Donovan would take her out the next day, and be thankful enough to annex such an attraction as a pretty girl. Various consequences would ensue and the long delay would be shortened; her mother's drawing room would resound with the clatter of teacups.

"Mrs. Bray's having some big thing next week; come with me there and I'll show you what I mane," Mrs. Donovan pleaded.

"I see what you mane," Rose answered, brushing away her temptation and getting up. "I'm much obliged to you."

"You know you're wrong, my dear," said her interlocutress, with angry little eyes.

"I'm not going to Mrs. Bray's."

"I'll get you a kyard; it'll only cost me a penny stamp."

"I've got one," said the girl, smiling.

"Do you mean a penny stamp?" Mrs. Donovan, especially at departure, always observed all the forms of amity. "You can't do it alone, my darling," she declared.

"Shall they call you a cab?" Rose asked.

"I'll pick one up. I choose my horse. You know you require your start," her visitor went on.

"Excuse my mother," was Rose's only reply.

"Don't mention it. Come to me when you need me. You'll find me in the Red Book."

"It's awfully kind of you."

Mrs. Donovan lingered a moment on the threshold. "Who will you *have* now, my child?" she appealed.

"I won't have anyone!" Rose turned away, blushing for her. "She came on speculation," she said afterwards to Mrs. Tramore.

Her mother looked at her a moment in silence. "You can do it if you like, you know."

Rose made no direct answer to this observation; she remarked instead: "See what our quiet life allows us to escape."

"We don't escape it. She has been here an hour."

"Once in twenty years! We might meet her three times a day."

"Oh, I'd take her with the rest!" sighed Mrs. Tramore; while her daughter recognized that what her companion wanted to do was just what Mrs. Donovan was doing. Mrs. Donovan's life was her ideal.

On a Sunday, ten days later, Rose went to see one of her old governesses, of whom she had lost sight for some time and who had written to her that she was in London, unoccupied and ill. This was just the sort of relation into which she could throw herself now with inordinate zeal; the idea of it, however, not preventing a foretaste of the queer expression in the excellent lady's face when she should mention with whom she was living. While she smiled at this picture she threw in another joke, asking herself if Miss Hack could be held in any degree to constitute the nucleus of a circle. She would come to see her, in any event – come the more the further she was dragged down. Sunday was always a difficult day with the two ladies – the afternoons made it so apparent that they were not frequented. Her mother, it is true, was comprised in the habits of two or three old gentlemen – she had for a long time avoided male friends of less than seventy – who disliked each other enough to make the room, when they were there at once, crack with pressure. Rose sat for a long time with Miss Hack, doing conscientious justice to the conception that there could be troubles in the world worse than her own; and when she came back her mother was alone, but with a story to tell of a long visit from Mr. Guy Mangler, who had waited and waited for her return. "He's in love with you; he's coming again on Tuesday," Mrs. Tramore announced.

"Did he say so?"

"That he's coming back on Tuesday?"

"No, that he's in love with me."

"He didn't need, when he stayed two hours."

"With you? It's you he's in love with, mamma!"

"That will do as well," laughed Mrs. Tramore. "For all the use we shall make of him!" she added in a moment.

"We shall make great use of him. His mother sent him."

"Oh, she'll never come!"

"Then *he* shan't," said Rose. Yet he was admitted on the Tuesday, and after she had given him his tea Mrs. Tramore left the young people alone. Rose wished she hadn't – she herself had another view. At any rate she disliked her mother's view, which she had easily guessed. Mr. Mangler did nothing but say how charming he thought his hostess of the Sunday, and what a tremendously jolly visit he had had. He didn't remark in so many words "I had no idea your mother was such a good sort"; but this was the spirit of his simple discourse. Rose liked it at first – a little of it gratified her; then she thought there was too much of it for good taste. She had to reflect that one does what one can and that Mr. Mangler probably thought he was delicate. He wished to convey that he desired to make up to her for the injustice of society. Why shouldn't her mother receive gracefully, she asked (not audibly) and who had ever said she didn't? Mr. Mangler had a great deal to say about the disappointment of his own parent over Miss Tramore's not having come to dine with them the night of his aunt's ball.

"Lady Maresfield knows why I didn't come," Rose answered at last.

"Ah, now, but *I* don't, you know; can't you tell *me?*" asked the young man.

"It doesn't matter, if your mother's clear about it."

"Oh, but why make such an awful mystery of it, when I'm dying to know?"

He talked about this, he chaffed her about it for the rest of his visit: he had at last found a topic after his own heart. If her mother considered that he might be the emblem of their redemption he was an engine of the most primitive construction. He stayed and stayed; he struck Rose as on the point of bringing out something for which he had not quite, as he would have said, the cheek. Sometimes she thought he was going to begin: "By the way, my mother told me to propose to you." At other moments he seemed charged with the admission: "I say, of course I really know what you're trying to do for her," nodding at the door: "therefore hadn't we better speak of it frankly, so that I can help you with my mother, and more particularly with my sister Gwendolen, who's the difficult one? The fact is, you see, they won't do anything for nothing. If you'll accept me they'll call, but they won't call without something 'down.'" Mr. Mangler departed without their speaking frankly, and Rose Tramore had a hot hour during which she almost entertained, vindictively, the project of "accepting" the limpid youth until after she should have got her mother into circulation. The cream of the vision was that she might break with him later. She could read that this was what her mother would have liked, but the next time he came the door was closed to him, and the next and the next.

In August there was nothing to do but to go abroad, with the sense on Rose's part that the battle was still all to fight; for a round of country visits was not in prospect, and English watering-places constituted one of the few subjects on which the girl had heard her mother express herself with disgust. Continental autumns had been indeed for years, one of the various forms of Mrs. Tramore's atonement, but Rose could only infer that such fruit as they had borne was bitter. The stony stare of Belgravia could be practiced at Homburg; and somehow it was inveterately only gentlemen who sat next to her at the table d'hôte at Cadenabbia. Gentlemen had never been of any use to Mrs. Tramore for getting back into society; they had only helped her effectually to get out of it. She once dropped, to her daughter, in a moralizing mood, the remark that it was astonishing how many of them one could know without its doing one any good. Fifty of them – even very clever ones – represented a value inferior to that of one stupid woman. Rose wondered at the offhand way in which her mother could talk of fifty clever men; it seemed to her that the whole world couldn't contain such a number. She had a somber sense that mankind must be dull and mean. These cogitations took place in a cold hotel, in an eternal Swiss rain, and they had a flat echo in the transalpine valleys, as the lonely ladies went vaguely down to the Italian lakes and cities. Rose guided their course, at moments, with a kind of aimless ferocity; she moved abruptly, feeling vulgar and hating their life, though destitute of any definite vision of another life that would have been open to her. She had set herself a task and she clung to it; but she appeared to herself despicably idle. She had succeeded in not going to Homburg waters, where London was trying to wash away some of its stains; that would be too staring an advertisement of their situation. The main difference in situations to her now was the difference of being more or less pitied, at the best an intolerable danger; so that the places she preferred were the unsuspicious ones. She wanted to triumph with contempt, not with submission.

One morning in September, coming with her mother out of the marble church at Milan, she perceived that a gentleman who had just passed her on his way into the cathedral and whose face she had not noticed, had quickly raised his hat, with a suppressed ejaculation. She involuntarily glanced back; the gentleman had paused, again uncovering, and Captain Jay stood saluting her in the Italian sunshine. "Oh, good-morning!" she said, and walked on, pursuing her course; her mother was a little in front. She overtook her in a moment, with an unreasonable sense, like a gust of cold air, that men were worse than ever, for Captain Jay had apparently moved into the church. Her mother turned as they met, and suddenly, as she looked back, an expression of peculiar sweetness came into this lady's eyes. It made Rose's take the same direction and rest a second time on Captain Jay, who was planted just where he had stood a minute before. He immediately came forward, asking Rose with great gravity if he might speak to her a moment, while Mrs. Tramore went her way again. He had the expression of a man who wished to say something very important; yet his next words were simple enough and consisted of the remark that he had not seen her for a year.

"Is it really so much as that?" asked Rose.

"Very nearly. I would have looked you up, but in the first place I have been very little in London, and in the second I believed it wouldn't have done any good."

"You should have put that first," said the girl. "It wouldn't have done any good."

He was silent over this a moment, in his customary deciphering way; but the view he took of it did not prevent him from inquiring, as she slowly followed her mother, if he mightn't walk with her now. She answered with a laugh that it wouldn't do any good but that he might do as he liked. He replied without the slightest manifestation of levity that it would do more good than if he didn't, and they strolled together, with Mrs. Tramore well before them, across the big, amusing piazza, where the front of the cathedral makes a sort of builded light. He asked a question or two and he explained his own presence: having a month's holiday, the first clear time for several years, he had just popped over the Alps. He inquired if Rose had recent news of the old lady in Hill Street, and it was the only tortuous thing she had ever heard him say.

"I have had no communication of any kind from her since I parted with you under her roof. Hasn't she mentioned that?" said Rose.

"I haven't seen her."

"I thought you were such great friends."

Bertram Jay hesitated a moment. "Well, not so much now."

"What has she done to you?" Rose demanded.

He fidgeted a little, as if he were thinking of something that made him unconscious of her question; then, with mild violence, he brought out the inquiry: "Miss Tramore, are you happy?"

She was startled by the words, for she on her side had been reflecting – reflecting that he had broken with her grandmother and that this pointed to a reason. It suggested at least that he wouldn't now be so much like a mouthpiece for that cold ancestral tone. She turned off his question – said it never was a fair one, as you gave yourself away however you answered it. When he repeated "You give yourself away?" as if he didn't understand, she remembered that he had not read the funny American books. This brought them to a silence, for she had enlightened him only by another laugh, and he was evidently preparing another question, which he wished carefully to disconnect from the former. Presently, just as they were coming near Mrs. Tramore, it arrived in the words "Is this lady your mother?" On Rose's assenting, with the addition that she was traveling with her, he said: "Will you be so kind as to introduce me to her?" They were so close to Mrs. Tramore that she probably heard, but she floated away with a single stroke of her paddle and an inattentive poise of her head. It was a striking exhibition of the famous tact, for Rose delayed to answer, which was exactly what might have made her mother wish to turn; and indeed when at last the girl spoke she only said to her companion: "Why do you ask me that?"

"Because I desire the pleasure of making her acquaintance."

Rose had stopped, and in the middle of the square they stood looking at each other. "Do you remember what you said to me the last time I saw you?"

"Oh, don't speak of that!"

"It's better to speak of it now than to speak of it later."

Bertram Jay looked round him, as if to see whether anyone would hear; but the bright foreignness gave him a sense of safety, and he unexpectedly exclaimed: "Miss Tramore, I love you more than ever!"

"Then you ought to have come to see us," declared the girl, quickly walking on.

"You treated me the last time as if I were positively offensive to you."

"So I did, but you know my reason."

"Because I protested against the course you were taking? I did, I did!" the young man rang out, as if he still, a little, stuck to that.

His tone made Rose say gaily: "Perhaps you do so yet?"

"I can't tell till I've seen more of your circumstances," he replied with eminent honesty.

The girl stared; her light laugh filled the air. "And it's in order to see more of them and judge that you wish to make my mother's acquaintance?"

He colored at this and he evaded; then he broke out with a confused "Miss Tramore, let me stay with you a little!" which made her stop again.

"Your company will do us great honor, but there must be a rigid condition attached to our acceptance of it."

"Kindly mention it," said Captain Jay, staring at the façade of the cathedral.

"You don't take us on trial."

"On trial?"

"You don't make an observation to me – not a single one, ever, ever! – on the matter that, in Hill Street, we had our last words about."

Captain Jay appeared to be counting the thousand pinnacles of the church. "I think you really must be right," he remarked at last.

"There you are!" cried Rose Tramore, and walked rapidly away.

He caught up with her, he laid his hand upon her arm to stay her. "If you're going to Venice, let me go to Venice with you!"

"You don't even understand my condition."

"I'm sure you're right, then: you must be right about everything."

"That's not in the least true, and I don't care a fig whether you're sure or not. Please let me go."

He had barred her way, he kept her longer. "I'll go and speak to your mother myself!"

Even in the midst of another emotion she was amused at the air of audacity accompanying this declaration. Poor Captain Jay might have been on the point of marching up to a battery. She looked at him a moment; then she said: "You'll be disappointed!"

"Disappointed?"

"She's much more proper than grandmamma, because she's much more amiable."

"Dear Miss Tramore – dear Miss Tramore!" the young man murmured helplessly.

"You'll see for yourself. Only there's another condition," Rose went on.

"Another?" he cried, with discouragement and alarm.

"You must understand thoroughly, before you throw in your lot with us even for a few days, what our position really is."

"Is it very bad?" asked Bertram Jay artlessly.

"No one has anything to do with us, no one speaks to us, no one looks at us."

"Really?" stared the young man.

"We've no social existence, we're utterly despised."

"Oh, Miss Tramore!" Captain Jay interposed. He added quickly, vaguely, and with a want of presence of mind of which he as quickly felt ashamed: "Do none of your family – ?" The question collapsed; the brilliant girl was looking at him.

"We're extraordinarily happy," she threw out.

"Now that's all I wanted to know!" he exclaimed, with a kind of exaggerated cheery reproach, walking on with her briskly to overtake her mother.

He was not dining at their inn, but he insisted on coming that evening to their table d'hôte. He sat next Mrs. Tramore, and in the evening he accompanied them gallantly to the opera, at a third-rate theater where they were almost the only ladies in the boxes. The next day they went together by rail to the Charterhouse of Pavia, and while he strolled with the girl, as they waited for the homeward train, he said to her candidly: "Your mother's remarkably pretty." She remembered the words and the feeling they gave her: they were the first note of new era. The feeling was somewhat that of an anxious, gratified matron who has "presented" her child and is thinking of the matrimonial market. Men might be of no use, as Mrs. Tramore said, yet it was from this moment Rose dated the rosy dawn of her confidence that her protégée would go off; and when later, in crowded assemblies, the phrase, or something like it behind a hat or a fan, fell repeatedly on her anxious ear, "Your mother *is* in beauty!" or "I've never seen her look better!" she had a faint vision of the yellow sunshine and the afternoon shadows on the dusty Italian platform.

Mrs. Tramore's behavior at this period was a revelation of her native understanding of delicate situations. She needed no account of this one from her daughter – it was one of the things for which she had a scent; and there was a kind of loyalty to the rules of a game in the silent sweetness with which she smoothed the path of Bertram Jay. It was clear that she was in her element in fostering the exercise of the affections, and if she ever spoke without thinking twice it is probable that she would have exclaimed, with some gaiety, "Oh, I know all about *love!*" Rose could see that she thought their companion would be a help, in spite of his being no dispenser of patronage. The key to the gates of fashion had not been placed in his hand, and no one had ever heard of the ladies of his family, who lived in some vague hollow of the Yorkshire moors; but nonetheless he might administer a muscular push. Yes indeed, men in general were broken reeds, but Captain Jay was peculiarly representative. Respectability was the woman's maximum, as honor was the man's, but this distinguished young soldier inspired more than one kind of confidence. Rose had a great deal of attention for the use to which his respectability was put; and there mingled with this attention some amusement and much compassion. She saw that after a couple of days he decidedly liked her mother, and that he was yet not in the least aware of it. He took for granted that he believed in her but little; notwithstanding which he would have trusted her with anything except Rose herself. His trusting her with Rose would come very soon. He never spoke to her daughter about her qualities of character, but two or three of them (and indeed these were all the poor lady had, and they made the best show) were what he had in mind in praising her appearance. When he remarked: "What attention Mrs. Tramore seems to attract everywhere!" he meant: "What a beautifully simple nature it is!" and when he said: "There's something extraordinarily harmonious in the colors she wears," it signified: "Upon my word, I never saw such a sweet temper in my life!" She lost one of her boxes at Verona, and made the prettiest joke of it to Captain Jay. When Rose saw this she said to herself, "Next season we shall have only to choose." Rose knew what was in the box.

By the time they reached Venice (they had stopped at half a dozen little old romantic cities in the most frolicsome aesthetic way) she liked their companion better than she had ever liked him before. She did him the justice to recognize that if he was not quite honest with himself he was at least wholly honest with *her.* She reckoned up everything he had been since he joined them, and put upon it all an interpretation so favorable to his devotion that, catching herself in the act of glossing over one or two episodes that had not struck her at the time as disinterested she exclaimed, beneath her breath, "Look out – you're falling in love!" But if he liked correctness wasn't he quite right? Could anyone possibly like it more than *she* did? And if he had protested against her throwing in her lot with her mother, this was not because of the benefit conferred but because of the injury received. He exaggerated that injury, but this was the privilege of a lover perfectly willing to be selfish on behalf of his mistress. He might have wanted her grandmother's money for her, but if he had given her up on first discovering that she was throwing away her chance of it (oh, this was *her* doing too!) he had given up her grandmother as much: not keeping well with the old woman, as some men would have done; not waiting to see how the perverse experiment would turn out and appeasing her, if it should promise tolerably, with a view to future operations. He had had a simple-minded, evangelical, lurid view of what the girl he loved would find herself in for. She could see this now – she could see it from his present bewilderment and mystification, and she liked him and pitied him, with the kindest smile, for the original naïveté as well as for the actual meekness. No wonder he hadn't known what she was in for, since he now didn't even know what he was in for himself. Were there not moments when he thought his companions almost unnaturally good, almost suspiciously safe? He had lost all power to verify that sketch of their isolation and declassement to which she had treated him on the great square at Milan. The last thing he noticed was that they were neglected, and he had never, for himself, had such an impression of society.

It could scarcely be enhanced even by the apparition of a large, fair, hot, red-haired young man, carrying a lady's fan in his hand, who suddenly stood before their little party as, on the third evening after their arrival in Venice, it partook of ices at one of the tables before the celebrated Café Florian. The lamplit Venetian dusk appeared to have revealed them to this gentleman as he sat with other friends at a neighboring table, and he had sprung up, with unsophisticated glee, to shake hands with Mrs. Tramore and her daughter. Rose recalled him to her mother, who looked at first as though she didn't remember him but presently bestowed a sufficiently gracious smile on Mr. Guy Mangler. He gave with youthful candor the history of his movements and indicated the whereabouts of his family: he was with his mother and sisters; they had met the Bob Veseys, who had taken Lord Whiteroy's yacht and were going to Constantinople. His mother and the girls, poor things, were at the Grand Hotel, but he was on the yacht with the Veseys, where they had Lord Whiteroy's cook. Wasn't the food in Venice filthy, and wouldn't they come and look at the yacht? She wasn't very fast, but she was awfully jolly. His mother might have come if she would, but she wouldn't at first, and now, when she wanted to, there were other people, who naturally wouldn't turn out for her. Mr. Mangler sat down; he alluded with artless resentment to the way, in July, the door of his friends had been closed to him. He was going to Constantinople, but he didn't care – if *they* were going anywhere; meanwhile his mother hoped awfully they would look her up.

Lady Maresfield, if she had given her son any such message, which Rose disbelieved, entertained her hope in a manner compatible with her sitting for half an hour, surrounded by her little retinue, without glancing in the direction of Mrs. Tramore. The girl, however, was aware that this was not a good enough instance of their humiliation; inasmuch as it was rather she who, on the occasion of their last contact, had held off from Lady Maresfield. She was a little ashamed now of not having answered the note in which this affable personage ignored her mother. She couldn't help perceiving indeed a dim movement on the part of some of the other members of the group; she made out an attitude of observation in the high-plumed head of Mrs. Vaughan-Vesey. Mrs. Vesey, perhaps, might have been looking at Captain Jay, for as this gentleman walked back to the hotel with our young lady (they were at the "Britannia," and young Mangler, who clung to them, went in front with Mrs. Tramore) he revealed to Rose that he had some acquaintance with Lady Maresfield's eldest daughter, though he didn't know and didn't particularly want to know, her ladyship. He expressed himself with more acerbity than she had ever heard him use (Christian charity so generally governed his speech) about the young donkey who had been prattling to them. They separated at the door of the hotel. Mrs. Tramore had got rid of Mr. Mangler, and Bertram Jay was in other quarters.

"If you know Mrs. Vesey, why didn't you go and speak to her? I'm sure she saw you," Rose said.

Captain Jay replied even more circumspectly than usual. "Because I didn't want to leave you."

"Well, you can go now; you're free," Rose rejoined.

"Thank you. I shall never go again."

"That won't be civil," said Rose.

"I don't care to be civil. I don't like her."

"Why don't you like her?"

"You ask too many questions."

"I know I do," the girl acknowledged.

Captain Jay had already shaken hands with her, but at this he put out his hand again. "She's too worldly," he murmured, while he held Rose Tramore's a moment.

"Ah, you dear!" Rose exclaimed almost audibly as, with her mother, she turned away.

The next morning, upon the Grand Canal, the gondola of our three friends encountered a stately barge which, though it contained several persons, seemed pervaded mainly by one majestic presence. During the instant the gondolas were passing each other it was impossible either for Rose Tramore or for her companions not to become conscious that this distinguished identity had markedly inclined itself—a circumstance commemorated the next moment, almost within earshot of the other boat, by the most spontaneous cry that had issued for many a day from the lips of Mrs. Tramore. "Fancy, my dear, Lady Maresfield has bowed to us!"

"We ought to have returned it," Rose answered; but she looked at Bertram Jay, who was opposite to her. He blushed, and she blushed, and during this moment was born a deeper understanding than had yet existed between these associated spirits. It had something to do with their going together that afternoon, without her mother, to look at certain out-of-the-way pictures as to which Ruskin had inspired her with a desire to see sincerely. Mrs. Tramore expressed the wish to stay at home, and the motive of this wish – a finer shade than any that even Ruskin had ever found a phrase for – was not translated into misrepresenting words by either the mother or the daughter. At San Giovanni in Bragora the girl and her companion came upon Mrs. Vaughan-Vesey, who, with one of her sisters, was also endeavoring to do the earnest thing. She did it to Rose, she did it to Captain Jay, as well as to Gianbellini; she was a handsome, long-necked, aquiline person, of a different type from the rest of her family, and she did it remarkably well. She secured our friends – it was her own expression – for luncheon, on the morrow, on the yacht, and she made it public to Rose that she would come that afternoon to invite her mother. When the girl returned to the hotel, Mrs. Tramore mentioned, before Captain Jay, who had come up to their sitting room, that Lady Maresfield had called. "She stayed a long time – at least it seemed long!" laughed Mrs. Tramore.

The poor lady could laugh freely now; yet there was some grimness in a colloquy that she had with her daughter after Bertram Jay had departed. Before this happened Mrs. Vesey's card, scrawled over in pencil and referring to the morrow's luncheon, was brought up to Mrs. Tramore.

"They mean it all as a bribe," said the principal recipient of these civilities.

"As a bribe?" Rose repeated.

"She wants to marry you to that boy; they've seen Captain Jay and they're frightened."

"Well, dear mamma, I can't take Mr. Mangler for a husband."

"Of course not. But oughtn't we to go to the luncheon?"

"Certainly we'll go to the luncheon," Rose said; and when the affair took place, on the morrow, she could feel for the first time that she was taking her mother out. This appearance was somehow brought home to everyone else, and it was really the agent of her success. For it is of the essence of this simple history that, in the first place, that success dated from Mrs. Vesey's Venetian dejeuner, and in the second reposed, by a subtle social logic, on the very anomaly that had made it dubious. There is always a chance in things, and Rose Tramore's chance was in the fact that Gwendolen Vesey was, as someone had said, awfully modern, an immense improvement on the exploded science of her mother, and capable of seeing what a "draw" there would be in the comedy, if properly brought out, of the reversed positions of Mrs. Tramore and Mrs. Tramore's diplomatic daughter. With a first-rate managerial eye she perceived that people would flock into any room – and all the more into one of hers – to see Rose bring in her dreadful mother. She treated the cream of English society to this thrilling spectacle later in the autumn, when she once more "secured" both the performers for a week at Brimble. It made a hit on the spot, the very first evening – the girl was felt to play her part so well. The rumor of the performance spread; everyone wanted to see it. It was an entertainment of which, that winter in the country, and the next season in town, persons of taste desired to give their friends the freshness. The thing was to make the Tramores come late, after everyone had arrived. They were engaged for a fixed hour, like the American imitator and the Patagonian contralto. Mrs. Vesey had been the first to say the girl was awfully original, but that became the general view.

Gwendolen Vesey had with her mother one of the few quarrels in which Lady Maresfield had really stood up to such an antagonist (the elder woman had to recognize in general in whose veins it was that the blood of the Manglers flowed) on account of this very circumstance of her attaching more importance to Miss Tramore's originality ("Her originality be hanged!" her ladyship had gone so far as unintelligently to exclaim) than to the prospects of the unfortunate Guy. Mrs. Vesey actually lost sight of these pressing problems in her admiration of the way the mother and the daughter, or rather the daughter and the mother (it was slightly confusing) "drew." It was Lady Maresfield's version of the case that the brazen girl (she was shockingly coarse) had treated poor Guy abominably. At any rate it was made known, just after Easter, that Miss Tramore was to be married to Captain Jay. The marriage was not to take place till the summer; but Rose felt that before this the field would practically be won. There had been some bad moments, there had been several warm corners and a certain number of cold shoulders and closed doors and stony stares; but the breach was effectually made – the rest was only a question of time. Mrs. Tramore could be trusted to keep what she had gained, and it was the dowagers, the old dragons with prominent fangs and glittering scales, whom the trick had already mainly caught. By this time there were several houses into which the liberated lady had crept alone. Her daughter had been expected with her, but they couldn't turn her out because the girl had stayed behind, and she was fast acquiring a new identity, that of a parental connection with the heroine of such a romantic story. She was at least the next best thing to her daughter, and Rose foresaw the day when she would be valued principally as a memento of one of the prettiest episodes in the annals of London. At a big official party, in June, Rose had the joy of introducing Eric to his mother. She was a little sorry it was an official party – there were some other such queer people there; but Eric called, observing the shade, the next day but one.

No observer, probably, would have been acute enough to fix exactly the moment at which the girl ceased to take out her mother and began to be taken out by her. A later phase was more distinguishable – that at which Rose forbore to inflict on her companion a duality that might become oppressive. She began to economize her force, she went only when the particular effect was required. Her marriage was delayed by the period of mourning consequent upon the death of her grandmother, who, the younger Mrs. Tramore averred, was killed by the rumor of her own new birth. She was the only one of the dragons who had not been tamed. Julia Tramore knew the truth about this – she was determined such things should not kill *her*. She would live to do something – she hardly knew what. The provisions of her mother's will were published in the "Illustrated News"; from which it appeared that everything that was not to go to Eric and to Julia was to go to the fortunate Edith. Miss Tramore makes no secret of her own intentions as regards this favorite.

Edith is not pretty, but Lady Maresfield is waiting for her; she is determined Gwendolen Vesey shall not get hold of her. Mrs. Vesey however takes no interest in her at all. She is whimsical, as befits a woman of her fashion; but there are two persons she is still very fond of, the delightful Bertram Jays. The fondness of this pair, it must be added, is not wholly expended in return. They are extremely united, but their life is more domestic than might have been expected from the preliminary signs. It owes a portion of its concentration to the fact that Mrs. Tramore has now so many places to go to that she has almost no time to come to her daughter's. She is, under her son-in-law's roof, a brilliant but a rare apparition, and the other day he remarked upon the circumstance to his wife.

"If it hadn't been for you," she replied, smiling, "she might have had her regular place at our fireside."

"Good heavens, how did I prevent it?" cried Captain Jay, with all the consciousness of virtue.

"You ordered it otherwise, you goose!" And she says, in the same spirit, whenever her husband commends her (which he does, sometimes, extravagantly) for the way she launched her mother: "Nonsense, my dear – practically it was *you!*"

Greville Fane

Coming in to dress for dinner, I found a telegram: "Mrs. Stormer dying; can you give us half a column for tomorrow evening? Let her off easy, but not too easy." I was late; I was in a hurry; I had very little time to think, but at a venture I dispatched a reply: "Will do what I can." It was not till I had dressed and was rolling away to dinner that, in the hansom, I bethought myself of the difficulty of the condition attached. The difficulty was not of course in letting her off easy but in qualifying that indulgence. "I simply won't qualify it," I said to myself. I didn't admire her, but I liked her, and I had known her so long that I almost felt heartless in sitting down at such an hour to a feast of indifference. I must have seemed abstracted, for the early years of my acquaintance with her came back to me. I spoke of her to the lady I had taken down, hut the lady I had taken down had never heard of Greville Fane. I tried my other neighbor, who pronounced her books "too vile." I had never thought them very good, but I should let her off easier than that.

I came away early, for the express purpose of driving to ask about her. The journey took time, for she lived in the northwest district, in the neighborhood of Primrose Hill. My apprehension that I should be too late was justified in a fuller sense than I had attached to it – I had only feared that the house would be shut up. There were lights in the windows, and the temperate tinkle of my bell brought a servant immediately to the door, but poor Mrs. Stormer had passed into a state in which the resonance of no earthly knocker was to be feared. A lady, in the hall, hovering behind the servant, came forward when she heard my voice. I recognized Lady Luard, but she had mistaken me for the doctor.

"Excuse my appearing at such an hour," I said; "it was the first possible moment after I heard."

"It's all over," Lady Luard replied. "Dearest mamma!"

She stood there under the lamp with her eyes on me; she was very tall, very stiff, very cold, and always looked as if these things, and some others beside, in her dress, her manner and even her name, were an implication that she was very admirable. I had never been able to follow the argument, but that is a detail. I expressed briefly and frankly what I felt, while the little mottled maidservant flattened herself against the wall of the narrow passage and tried to look detached without looking indifferent. It was not a moment to make a visit, and I was on the point of retreating when Lady Luard arrested me with a queer, casual, drawling "Would you – a – would you, perhaps, be *writing* something?" I felt for the instant like an interviewer, which I was not. But I pleaded guilty to this intention, on which she rejoined: "I'm so very glad – but I think my brother would like to see you." I detested her brother, but it wasn't an occasion to act this out; so I suffered myself to be inducted, to my surprise, into a small back room which I immediately recognized as the scene, during the later years, of Mrs. Stormer's imperturbable industry. Her table was there, the battered and blotted accessory to innumerable literary lapses, with its contracted space for the arms (she wrote only from the elbow down) and the confusion of scrappy, scribbled sheets which had already become literary remains. Leolin was also there, smoking a cigarette before the fire and looking impudent even in his grief, sincere as it well might have been.

To meet him, to greet him, I had to make a sharp effort; for the air that he wore to me as he stood before me was quite that of his mother's murderer. She lay silent forever upstairs – as dead as an unsuccessful book, and his swaggering erectness was a kind of symbol of his having killed her. I wondered if he had already, with his sister, been calculating what they could get for the poor papers on the table; but I had not long to wait to learn, for in reply to the scanty words of sympathy I addressed him he puffed out: "It's miserable, miserable, yes; but she has left three books complete." His words had the oddest effect; they converted the cramped little room into a seat of trade and made the "book" wonderfully feasible. He would certainly get all that could be got for the three. Lady Luard explained to me that her husband had been with them but had had to go down to the House. To her brother she explained that I was going to write something, and to me again she made it clear that she hoped I would "do mamma justice." She added that she didn't think this had ever been done. She said to her brother: "Don't you think there are some things he ought thoroughly to understand?" and on his instantly exclaiming "Oh, thoroughly – thoroughly!" she went on, rather austerely: "I mean about mamma's birth."

"Yes, and her connections," Leolin added.

I professed every willingness, and for five minutes I listened, but it would be too much to say that I understood. I don't even now, but it is not important. My vision was of other matters than those they put before me, and while they desired there should be no mistake about their ancestors I became more and more lucid about themselves. I got away as soon as possible, and walked home through the great dusky, empty London – the best of all conditions for thought. By the time I reached my door my little article was practically composed – ready to be transferred on the morrow from the polished plate of fancy. I believe it attracted some notice, was thought "graceful" and was said to be by someone else. I had to be pointed without being lively, and it took some tact. But what I said was much less interesting than what I thought – especially during the half-hour I spent in my armchair by the fire, smoking the cigar I always light before going to bed. I went to sleep there, I believe; but I continued to moralize about Greville Fane. I am reluctant to lose that retrospect altogether, and this is a dim little memory of it, a document not to "serve." The dear woman had written a hundred stories, but none so curious as her own.

When first I knew her she had published half-a-dozen fictions, and I believe I had also perpetrated a novel. She was more than a dozen years older than I, but she was a person who always acknowledged her relativity. It was not so very long ago, but in London, amid the big waves of the present, even a near horizon gets hidden. I met her at some dinner and took her down, rather flattered at offering my arm to a celebrity. She didn't look like one, with her matronly, mild, inanimate face, but I supposed her greatness would come out in her conversation. I gave it all the opportunities I could, but I was not disappointed when I found her only a dull, kind woman. This was why I liked her – she rested me so from literature. To myself literature was an irritation, a torment; but Greville Fane slumbered in the intellectual part of it like a Creole in a hammock. She was not a woman of genius, but her faculty was so special, so much a gift out of hand, that I have often wondered why she fell below that distinction. This was doubtless because the transaction, in her case, had remained incomplete; genius always pays for the gift, feels the debt, and she was placidly unconscious of obligation. She could invent stories by the yard, but she couldn't write a page of English. She went down to her grave without suspecting that though she had contributed volumes to the diversion of her contemporaries she had not contributed a sentence to the language. This had not prevented bushels of criticism from being heaped upon her head; she was worth a couple of columns any day to the weekly papers, in which it was shown that her pictures of life were dreadful but her style really charming. She asked me to come and see her, and I went. She lived then in Montpellier Square; which helped me to see how dissociated her imagination was from her character.

An industrious widow, devoted to her daily stint, to meeting the butcher and baker and making a home for her son and daughter, from the moment she took her pen in her hand she became a creature of passion. She thought the English novel deplorably wanting in that element, and the task she had cut out for herself was to supply the deficiency. Passion in high life was the general formula of this work, for her imagination was at home only in the most exalted circles. She adored, in truth, the aristocracy, and they constituted for her the romance of the world or, what is more to the point, the prime material of fiction. Their beauty and luxury, their loves and revenges, their temptations and surrenders, their immoralities and diamonds were as familiar to her as the blots on her writing-table. She was not a belated producer of the old fashionable novel, she had a cleverness and a modernness of her own, she had freshened up the fly-blown tinsel. She turned off plots by the hundred and – so far as her flying quill could convey her – was perpetually going abroad. Her types, her illustrations, her tone were nothing if not cosmopolitan. She recognized nothing less provincial than European society, and her fine folk knew each other and made love to each other from Doncaster to Bucharest. She had an idea that she resembled Balzac, and her favorite historical characters were Lucien de Rubempre and the Vidame de Pamiers. I must add that when I once asked her who the latter personage was she was unable to tell me. She was very brave and healthy and cheerful, very abundant and innocent and wicked. She was clever and vulgar and snobbish, and never so intensely British as when she was particularly foreign.

This combination of qualities had brought her early success, and I remember having heard with wonder and envy of what she "got," in those days, for a novel. The revelation gave me a pang: it was such a proof that, practicing a totally different style, I should never make my fortune. And yet when, as I knew her better she told me her real tariff and I saw how rumor had quadrupled it, I liked her enough to be sorry. After a while I discovered too that if she got less it was not that *I* was to get anymore. My failure never had what Mrs. Stormer would have called the banality of being relative – it was always admirably absolute. She lived at ease however in those days – ease is exactly the word, though she produced three novels a year. She scorned me when I spoke of difficulty – it was the only thing that made her angry. If I hinted that a work of art required a tremendous licking into shape she thought it a pretension and a pose. She never recognized the "torment of form"; the furthest she went was to introduce into one of her books (in satire her hand was heavy) a young poet who was always talking about it. I couldn't quite understand her irritation on this score, for she had nothing at stake in the matter. She had a shrewd perception that form, in prose at least, never recommended anyone to the public we were condemned to address, and therefore she lost nothing (putting her private humiliation aside) by not having any. She made no pretence of producing works of art, but had comfortable tea-drinking hours in which she freely confessed herself a common pastry cook, dealing in such tarts and puddings as would bring customers to the shop. She put in plenty of sugar and of cochineal, or whatever it is that gives these articles a rich and attractive color. She had a serene superiority to observation and opportunity which constituted an inexpugnable strength and would enable her to go on indefinitely. It is only real success that wanes, it is only solid things that melt. Greville Fane's ignorance of life was a resource still more unfailing than the most approved receipt. On her saying once that the day would come when she should have written herself out I answered: "Ah, you look into fairyland, and the fairies love you, and *they* never change. Fairyland is always there; it always was from the beginning of time, and it always will be to the end. They've given you the key and you can always open the door. With me it's different; I try, in my clumsy way, to be in some direct relation to life." "Oh, bother your direct relation to life!" she used to reply, for she was always annoyed by the phrase – which would not in the least prevent her from using it when she wished to try for style. With no more prejudices than an old sausage-mill, she would give forth again with patient punctuality any poor verbal scrap that had been dropped into her. I cheered her with saying that the dark day, at the end, would be for the like of *me;* inasmuch as, going in our small way by experience and observation, we depended not on a revelation, but on a little tiresome process. Observation depended on opportunity, and where should we be when opportunity failed?

One day she told me that as the novelist's life was so delightful and during the good years at least such a comfortable support (she had these staggering optimisms) she meant to train up her boy to follow it. She took the ingenious view that it was a profession like another and that therefore everything was to be gained by beginning young and serving an apprenticeship. Moreover the education would be less expensive than any other special course, inasmuch as she could administer it herself. She didn't profess to keep a school, but she could at least teach her own child. It was not that she was so very clever, but (she confessed to me as if she were afraid I would laugh at her) that *he* was. I didn't laugh at her for that, for I thought the boy sharp – I had seen him at sundry times. He was well grown and good-looking and unabashed, and both he and his sister made me wonder about their defunct papa, concerning whom the little I knew was that he had been a clergyman. I explained them to myself by suppositions and imputations possibly unjust to the departed; so little were they – superficially at least – the children of their mother. There used to be, on an easel in her drawing room, an enlarged photograph of her husband, done by some horrible posthumous "process" and draped, as to its florid frame, with a silken scarf, which testified to the candor of Greville Fane's bad taste. It made him look like an unsuccessful tragedian; but it was not a thing to trust. He may have been a successful comedian. Of the two children the girl was the elder, and struck me in all her younger years as singularly colorless. She was only very long, like an undecipherable letter. It was not till Mrs. Stormer came back from a protracted residence abroad that Ethel (which was this young lady's name) began to produce the effect, which was afterwards remarkable in her, of a certain kind of high resolution. She made one apprehend that she meant to do something for herself. She was long-necked and near-sighted and striking, and I thought I had never seen sweet seventeen in a form so hard and high and dry. She was cold and affected and ambitious, and she carried an eyeglass with a long handle, which she put up whenever she wanted not to see. She had come out, as the phrase is, immensely; and yet I felt as if she were surrounded with a spiked iron railing. What she meant to do for herself was to marry, and it was the only thing, I think, that she meant to do for anyone else; yet who would be inspired to clamber over that bristling barrier? What flower of tenderness or of intimacy would such an adventurer conceive as his reward?

This was for Sir Baldwin Luard to say; but he naturally never confided to me the secret. He was a joyless, jokeless young man, with the air of having other secrets as well, and a determination to get on politically that was indicated by his never having been known to commit himself – as regards any proposition whatever – beyond an exclamatory "Oh!" His wife and he must have conversed mainly in prim ejaculations, but they understood sufficiently that they were kindred spirits. I remember being angry with Greville Fane when she announced these nuptials to me as magnificent; I remember asking her what splendor there was in the union of the daughter of a woman of genius with an irredeemable mediocrity. "Oh! he's awfully clever," she said; but she blushed for the maternal fib. What she meant was that though Sir Baldwin's estates were not vast (he had a dreary house in South Kensington and a still drearier "Hall" somewhere in Essex, which was let), the connection was a "smarter" one than a child of hers could have aspired to form. In spite of the social bravery of her novels she took a very humble and dingy view of herself, so that of all her productions "my daughter Lady Luard" was quite the one she was proudest of. That personage thought her mother very vulgar and was distressed and perplexed by the occasional license of her pen, but had a complicated attitude in regard to this indirect connection with literature. So far as it was lucrative her ladyship approved of it, and could compound with the inferiority of the pursuit by doing practical justice to some of its advantages. I had reason to know (my reason was simply that poor Mrs. Stormer told me) that she suffered the inky fingers to press an occasional bank-note into her palm. On the other hand she deplored the "peculiar style" to which Greville Fane had devoted herself, and wondered where an author who had the convenience of so ladylike a daughter could have picked up such views about the best society. "She might know better, with Leolin and me," Lady Luard had been known to remark; but it appeared that some of Greville Fane's superstitions were incurable. She didn't live in Lady Luard's society, and the best was not good enough for her – she must make it still better.

I could see that this necessity grew upon her during the years she spent abroad, when I had glimpses of her in the shifting sojourns that lay in the path of my annual ramble. She betook herself from Germany to Switzerland and from Switzerland to Italy; she favored cheap places and set up her desk in the smaller capitals. I took a look at her whenever I could, and I always asked how Leolin was getting on. She gave me beautiful accounts of him, and whenever it was possible the boy was produced for my edification. I had entered from the first into the joke of his career – I pretended to regard him as a consecrated child. It had been a joke for Mrs. Stormer at first, but the boy himself had been shrewd enough to make the matter serious. If his mother accepted the principle that the intending novelist cannot begin too early to see life, Leolin was not interested in hanging back from the application of it. He was eager to qualify himself, and took to cigarettes at ten, on the highest literary grounds. His poor mother gazed at him with extravagant envy and, like Desdemona, wished heaven had made *her* such a man. She explained to me more than once that in her profession she had found her sex a dreadful drawback. She loved the story of Madame George Sand's early rebellion against this hindrance, and believed that if she had worn trousers she could have written as well as that lady. Leolin had for the career at least the qualification of trousers, and as he grew older he recognized its importance by laying in an immense assortment. He grew up in gorgeous apparel, which was his way of interpreting his mother's system. Whenever I met her I found her still under the impression that she was carrying this system out and that Leolin's training was bearing fruit. She was giving him experience, she was giving him impressions, she was putting a gagnepain into his hand. It was another name for spoiling him with the best conscience in the world. The queerest pictures come back to me of this period of the good lady's life and of the extraordinarily virtuous, muddled, bewildering tenor of it. She had an idea that she was seeing foreign manners as well as her petticoats would allow; but, in reality she was not seeing anything, least of all fortunately how much she was laughed at. She drove her whimsical pen at Dresden and at Florence, and produced in all places and at all times the same romantic and ridiculous fictions. She carried about her box of properties and fished out promptly the familiar, tarnished old puppets. She believed in them when others couldn't, and as they were like nothing that was to be seen under the sun it was impossible to prove by comparison that they were wrong. You can't compare birds and fishes; you could only feel that, as Greville Fane's characters had the fine plumage of the former species, human beings must be of the latter.

It would have been droll if it had not been so exemplary to see her tracing the loves of the duchesses beside the innocent cribs of her children. The immoral and the maternal lived together in her diligent days on the most comfortable terms, and she stopped curling the mustaches of her Guardsmen to pat the heads of her babes. She was haunted by solemn spinsters who came to tea from continental pensions, and by unsophisticated Americans who told her she was just loved in *their* country. "I had rather be just paid there," she usually replied; for this tribute of transatlantic opinion was the only thing that galled her. The Americans went away thinking her coarse; though as the author of so many beautiful love-stories she was disappointing to most of these pilgrims, who had not expected to find a shy, stout, ruddy lady in a cap like a crumbled pyramid. She wrote about the affections and the impossibility of controlling them, but she talked of the price of pension and the convenience of an English chemist. She devoted much thought and many thousands of francs to the education of her daughter, who spent three years at a very superior school at Dresden, receiving wonderful instruction in sciences, arts and tongues, and who, taking a different line from Leolin, was to be brought up wholly as a *femme du monde.* The girl was musical and philological; she made a specialty of languages and learned enough about them to be inspired with a great contempt for her mother's artless accents. Greville Fane's French and Italian were droll; the imitative faculty had been denied her, and she had an unequaled gift, especially pen in hand, of squeezing big mistakes into small opportunities. She knew it, but she didn't care; correctness was the virtue in the world that, like her heroes and heroines, she valued least. Ethel, who had perceived in her pages some remarkable lapses, undertook at one time to revise her proofs; but I remember her telling me a year after the girl had left school that this function had been very briefly exercised. "She can't read me," said Mrs. Stormer; "I offend her taste. She tells me that at Dresden – at school – I was never allowed." The good lady seemed surprised at this, having the best conscience in the world about her lucubrations. She had never meant to fly in the face of anything, and considered that she groveled before the Rhadamanthus of the English literary tribunal, the celebrated and awful Young Person. I assured her, as a joke, that she was frightfully indecent (she hadn't in fact that reality anymore than any other) my purpose being solely to prevent her from guessing that her daughter had dropped her not because she was immoral but because she was vulgar. I used to figure her children closeted together and asking each other while they exchanged a gaze of dismay: "Why should she *be* so – and so *fearfully* so – when she has the advantage of our society? Shouldn't *we* have taught her better?" Then I imagined their recognizing with a blush and a shrug that she was unteachable, irreformable. Indeed she was, poor lady; but it is never fair to read by the light of taste things that were not written by it. Greville Fane had, in the topsy-turvy, a serene good faith that ought to have been safe from allusion, like a stutter or a faux pas.

She didn't make her son ashamed of the profession to which he was destined, however; she only made him ashamed of the way she herself exercised it. But he bore his humiliation much better than his sister, for he was ready to take for granted that he should one day restore the balance. He was a canny and far-seeing youth, with appetites and aspirations, and he had not a scruple in his composition. His mother's theory of the happy knack he could pick up deprived him of the wholesome discipline required to prevent young idlers from becoming cads. He had, abroad, a casual tutor and a snatch or two of a Swiss school, but no consecutive study, no prospect of a university or a degree. It may be imagined with what zeal, as the years went on, he entered into the pleasantry of there being no manual so important to him as the massive book of life. It was an expensive volume to peruse, but Mrs. Stormer was willing to lay out a sum in what she would have called her *premiers frais.* Ethel disapproved – she thought this education far too unconventional for an English gentleman. Her voice was for Eton and Oxford, or for any public school (she would have resigned herself) with the army to follow. But Leolin never was afraid of his sister, and they visibly disliked, though they sometimes agreed to assist, each other. They could combine to work the oracle – to keep their mother at her desk.

When she came back to England, telling me she had got all the continent could give her, Leolin was a broad-shouldered, red-faced young man, with an immense wardrobe and an extraordinary assurance of manner. She was fondly obstinate about her having taken the right course with him, and proud of all that he knew and had seen. He was now quite ready to begin, and a little while later she told me he *had* begun. He had written something tremendously clever, and it was coming out in the Cheapside. I believe it came out; I had no time to look for it; I never heard anything about it. I took for granted that if this contribution had passed through his mother's hands it had practically become a specimen of her own genius, and it was interesting to consider Mrs. Stormer's future in the light of her having to write her son's novels as well as her own. This was not the way she looked at it herself; she took the charming ground that he would help her to write hers. She used to tell me that he supplied passages of the greatest value to her own work – all sorts of technical things, about hunting and yachting and wine – that she couldn't be expected to get very straight. It was all so much practice for him and so much alleviation for her. I was unable to identify these pages, for I had long since ceased to "keep up" with Greville Fane; but I was quite able to believe that the wine-question had been put, by Leolin's good offices, on a better footing, for the dear lady used to mix her drinks (she was perpetually serving the most splendid suppers) in the queerest fashion. I could see that he was willing enough to accept a commission to look after that department. It occurred to me indeed, when Mrs. Stormer settled in England again, that by making a shrewd use of both her children she might be able to rejuvenate her style. Ethel had come back to gratify her young ambition, and if she couldn't take her mother into society she would at least go into it herself. Silently, stiffly, almost grimly, this young lady held up her head, clenched her long teeth, squared her lean elbows and made her way up the staircases she had elected. The only communication she ever made to me, the only effusion of confidence with which she ever honored me, was when she said: "I don't want to know the people mamma knows; I mean to know others." I took due note of the remark, for I was not one of the "others." I couldn't trace therefore the steps of her process; I could only admire it at a distance and congratulate her mother on the results. The results were that Ethel went to "big" parties and got people to take her. Some of them were people she had met abroad, and others were people whom the people she had met abroad had met. They ministered alike to Miss Ethel's convenience, and I wondered how she extracted so many favors without the expenditure of a smile. Her smile was the dimmest thing in the world, diluted lemonade, without sugar, and she had arrived precociously at social wisdom, recognizing that if she was neither pretty enough nor rich enough nor clever enough, she could at least in her muscular youth be rude enough. Therefore if she was able to tell her mother what really took place in the mansions of the great, give her notes to work from, the quill could be driven at home to better purpose and precisely at a moment when it would have to be more active than ever. But if she did tell, it would appear that poor Mrs. Stormer didn't believe. As regards many points this was not a wonder; at any rate I heard nothing of Greville Fane's having developed a new manner. She had only one manner from start to finish, as Leolin would have said.

She was tired at last, but she mentioned to me that she couldn't afford to pause. She continued to speak of Leolin's work as the great hope of their future (she had saved no money) though the young man wore to my sense an aspect more and more professional if you like, but less and less literary. At the end of a couple of years there was something monstrous in the impudence with which he played his part in the comedy. When I wondered how she could play *her* part I had to perceive that her good faith was complete and that what kept it so was simply her extravagant fondness. She loved the young impostor with a simple, blind, benighted love, and of all the heroes of romance who had passed before her eyes he was by far the most brilliant.

He was at any rate the most real – she could touch him, pay for him, suffer for him, worship him. He made her think of her princes and dukes, and when she wished to fix these figures in her mind's eye she thought of her boy. She had often told me she was carried away by her own creations, and she was certainly carried away by Leolin. He vivified, by potentialities at least, the whole question of youth and passion. She held, not unjustly, that the sincere novelist should feel the whole flood of life; she acknowledged with regret that she had not had time to feel it herself, and it was a joy to her that the deficiency might be supplied by the sight of the way it was rushing through this magnificent young man. She exhorted him, I suppose, to let it rush; she wrung her own flaccid little sponge into the torrent. I knew not what passed between them in her hours of tuition, but I gathered that she mainly impressed on him that the great thing was to live, because that gave you material. He asked nothing better; he collected material, and the formula served as a universal pretext. You had only to look at him to see that, with his rings and breastpins, his cross-barred jackets, his early embonpoint, his eyes that looked like imitation jewels, his various indications of a dense, full-blown temperament, his idea of life was singularly vulgar; but he was not so far wrong as that his response to his mother's expectations was not in a high degree practical. If she had imposed a profession on him from his tenderest years it was exactly a profession that he followed. The two were not quite the same, inasmuch as *his* was simply to live at her expense; but at least she couldn't say that he hadn't taken a line. If she insisted on believing in him he offered himself to the sacrifice. My impression is that her secret dream was that he should have a liaison with a countess, and he persuaded her without difficulty that he had one. I don't know what countesses are capable of, but I have a clear notion of what Leolin was.

He didn't persuade his sister, who despised him – she wished to work her mother in her own way, and I asked myself why the girl's judgment of him didn't make me like her better. It was because it didn't save her after all from a mute agreement with him to go halves. There were moments when I couldn't help looking hard into his atrocious young eyes, challenging him to confess his fantastic fraud and give it up. Not a little tacit conversation passed between us in this way, but he had always the best of it. If I said: "Oh, come now, with *me* you needn't keep it up; plead guilty, and I'll let you off," he wore the most ingenuous, the most candid expression, in the depths of which I could read: "Oh, yes, I know it exasperates you – that's just why I do it." He took the line of earnest inquiry, talked about Balzac and Flaubert, asked me if I thought Dickens *did* exaggerate and Thackeray *ought* to be called a pessimist. Once he came to see me, at his mother's suggestion he declared, on purpose to ask me how far, in my opinion, in the English novel, one really might venture to "go." He was not resigned to the usual pruderies – he suffered under them already. He struck out the brilliant idea that nobody knew how far we might go, for nobody had ever tried. Did I think *he* might safely try – would it injure his mother if he did? He would rather disgrace himself by his timidities than injure his mother, but certainly someone ought to try. Wouldn't *I* try – couldn't I be prevailed upon to look at it as a duty? Surely the ultimate point ought to be fixed – he was worried, haunted by the question. He patronized me unblushingly, made me feel like a foolish amateur, a helpless novice, inquired into my habits of work and conveyed to me that I was utterly *vieux jeu* and had not had the advantage of an early training. I had not been brought up from the germ, I knew nothing of life – didn't go at it on *his* system. He had dipped into French feuilletons and picked up plenty of phrases, and he made a much better show in talk than his poor mother, who never had time to read anything and could only be vivid with her pen. If I didn't kick him downstairs it was because he would have alighted on her at the bottom.

When she went to live at Primrose Hill I called upon her and found her weary and wasted. It had waned a good deal, the elation caused the year before by Ethel's marriage; the foam on the cup had subsided and there was a bitterness in the draught.

She had had to take a cheaper house and she had to work still harder to pay even for that. Sir Baldwin was obliged to be close; his charges were fearful, and the dream of her living with her daughter (a vision she had never mentioned to me) must be renounced. "I would have helped with things, and I could have lived perfectly in one room," she said; "I would have paid for everything, and – after all – I'm someone, ain't I? But I don't fit in, and Ethel tells me there are tiresome people she *must* receive. I can help them from here, no doubt, better than from there. She told me once, you know, what she thinks of my picture of life. 'Mamma, your picture of life is preposterous!' No doubt it is, but she's vexed with me for letting my prices go down; and I had to write three novels to pay for all her marriage cost me. I did it very well – I mean the outfit and the wedding; but that's why I'm here. At any rate she doesn't want a dingy old woman in her house. I should give it an atmosphere of literary glory, but literary glory is only the eminence of nobodies. Besides, she doubts my glory – she knows I'm glorious only at Peckham and Hackney. She doesn't want her friends to ask if I've never known nice people. She can't tell them I've never been in society. She tried to teach me better once, but I couldn't learn. It would seem too as if Peckham and Hackney had had enough of me; for (don't tell anyone!) I've had to take less for my last than I ever took for anything." I asked her how little this had been, not from curiosity, but in order to upbraid her, more disinterestedly than Lady Luard had done, for such concessions. She answered "I'm ashamed to tell you," and then she began to cry.

I had never seen her break down, and I was proportionately moved; she sobbed, like a frightened child, over the extinction of her vogue and the exhaustion of her vein. Her little workroom seemed indeed a barren place to grow flowers, and I wondered, in the after years (for she continued to produce and publish) by what desperate and heroic process she dragged them out of the soil. I remember asking her on that occasion what had become of Leolin, and how much longer she intended to allow him to amuse himself at her cost. She rejoined with spirit, wiping her eyes, that he was down at Brighton hard at work – he was in the midst of a novel – and that he *felt* life so, in all its misery and mystery, that it was cruel to speak of such experiences as a pleasure. "He goes beneath the surface," she said, "and he *forces* himself to look at things from which he would rather turn away. Do you call that amusing yourself? You should see his face sometimes! And he does it for me as much as for himself. He tells me everything – he comes home to me with his trouvailles. We are artists together, and to the artist all things are pure. I've often heard you say so yourself." The novel that Leolin was engaged in at Brighton was never published, but a friend of mine and of Mrs. Stormer's who was staying there happened to mention to me later that he had seen the young apprentice to fiction driving, in a dogcart, a young lady with a very pink face. When I suggested that she was perhaps a woman of title with whom he was conscientiously flirting my informant replied: "She is indeed, but do you know what her title is?" He pronounced it – it was familiar and descriptive – but I won't reproduce it here. I don't know whether Leolin mentioned it to his mother: she would have needed all the purity of the artist to forgive him. I hated so to come across him that in the very last years I went rarely to see her, though I knew that she had come pretty well to the end of her rope. I didn't want her to tell me that she had fairly to give her books away – I didn't want to see her cry. She kept it up amazingly, and every few months, at my club, I saw three new volumes, in green, in crimson, in blue, on the book-table that groaned with light literature. Once I met her at the Academy soiree, where you meet people you thought were dead, and she vouchsafed the information, as if she owed it to me in candor, that Leolin had been obliged to recognize insuperable difficulties in the question of *form,* he was so fastidious; so that she had now arrived at a definite understanding with him (it was such a comfort) that *she* would do the form if he would bring home the substance. That was now his position – he foraged for her in the great world at a salary. "He's my 'devil,' don't you see? as if I were a great lawyer: he gets up the case and I argue it." She mentioned further that in addition to his salary he was paid by the piece: he got so much for a striking character, so much for a pretty name, so much for a plot, so much for an incident, and had so much promised him if he would invent a new crime.

"He *has* invented one," I said, "and he's paid every day of his life."

"What is it?" she asked, looking hard at the picture of the year; "Baby's Tub," near which we happened to be standing.

I hesitated a moment. "I myself will write a little story about it, and then you'll see."

But she never saw; she had never seen anything, and she passed away with her fine blindness unimpaired. Her son published every scrap of scribbled paper that could be extracted from her table-drawers, and his sister quarreled with him mortally about the proceeds, which showed that she only wanted a pretext, for they cannot have been great. I don't know what Leolin lives upon, unless it be on a queer lady many years older than himself, whom he lately married. The last time I met him he said to me with his infuriating smile: "Don't you think we can go a little further still – just a little?" *He* really goes too far.